MW01120679

PAYBACK

ROBERT DURAN SERIES

RAMÓN DEL VILLAR, ESQ.

Inklings Publishing

Edited by Fern Brady

Editorial Services, Johnnie Bernhard 808-227-0682

Cover Art by Verstandt

Second US Edition
17 16 15 14 13 12 11 1 2 3 4 5 6 7 8 9 10

ISBN: 978-1-944428-01-3 Paperback by Inklings Publishing

❀ Created with Vellum

DEDICATION

IN MEMORY OF DAVID LOWSLEY

This edition of my novel is dedicated to David Lowsley, a great friend and dedicated student at the Agnes Haury Institute of Court Interpreter of the University of Arizona. David was an inspiration to everybody who knew him and always a pleasure to have around.

When he went on to be with the Lord, David was a student at the University of Arizona School of Law. He was 64 years of age and suffering a progressive neurological disease for which there was no cure, yet, he started and continued his studies to become an attorney and never missed class in spite of his medical problems.

A captain in the U.S. Marine Corps, a veteran of Vietnam, and a successful business executive and entrepreneur, David would have been a great trial lawyer and very much like the fictional character of my novel.

All of us who loved you will keep your memory in our hearts. Farewell and until we meet again, my friend!

Ramón del Villar

PROLOGUE

MEXICO CITY

The black, 7-series BMW that had been traveling at a very high rate of speed followed by two equally black sedans, a Lexus LS450 and a Mercedes S600, slowed down on Constituyentes Avenue, just across the street from Chapultepec Park in Mexico City, to turn into the underground parking of the sixteen-story building. The building, high by Mexico City standards where the risk of an earthquake is always present, had an unusual pentagonal shape.

The large metal doors opened electrically and the three black cars went down one story to stop at an elegant lobby that opened to a small parking garage accommodating not more than six or seven cars. The parking garage for the public and tenants was in an adjacent five-story structure. This garage was reserved for the owner of the building.

The automatic glass doors to the lobby opened and one of the two young and extremely fit-looking men, who had been sitting at the marble counter next to the entry, quickly went to the BMW. The Lexus and the Mercedes had proceeded directly to parking spaces and from each descended four well-dressed men, obviously bodyguards, who then approached the BMW, whose heavy armor plated door was being opened by the man from the lobby.

A tall, over 6'3", very blond man, with blue eyes and an athletic built, who appeared to be in his early fifties and dressed in the casual elegance of wool trousers, silk shirt and a cashmere sweater, got out of the car, turned to the bodyguards and said, "I will not need you guys until tomorrow morning, have a good night." The guards dispersed after nodding respectfully while the tall man entered the lobby and walked directly to the single elevator on that lobby.

The building had five elevator shafts but for all purposes only four elevators operated in the building. The central elevator shaft, which was this one, was the only elevator that would go all the way up to the sixteenth floor of the building and the only one that came down to this private parking garage on the basement, and its doors were operated only with a special key.

The other man at the marble counter had walked to the elevator and had opened the door, so as soon as the tall, blond man walked in, he pushed the penthouse button. The vary fast elevator went up and the door opened into a white marble lobby located next to the living room of the marvelously decorated penthouse. The assistant asked, "Will you be needing anything sir?"

"No," was the curt answer, and the other just nodded respectfully and closed the elevator door.

The tall man walked into the living room and went directly to a marble table that had a telephone with two rows of buttons and punched the button for his private voice mail.

He knew he had a message. The voice mail had automatically dialed his cell phone and he had checked it during one of the breaks in the meeting of several hours he had been attending, probably it would be more proper to say presiding, that Sunday all day long. But he had not erased the message, he wanted to get home and listen to it again at his leisure.

Once he dialed the code, the clear voice of a very young woman came out of the speakerphone excitedly saying, "Daddy, daddy, I love you, I love you! I'm the happiest girl in the world! I am going to marry Manolo! Sorry I missed you, I'll tell you all later!

The hard face of the man softened with the happiness reflected in the voice of his only child and a small smile parted his lips. He pushed a couple of buttons and a recording device somewhere downstairs recorded the message while he repeated it to listen to it again. While he was listening, he pushed a button in a small console next to the telephone and the draperies covering the wall-size window opened to reveal an incredible view of Chapultepec Castle sitting atop the mountain of the crickets. It seemed like if he could touch the castle from where he was standing.

'So Manolito will act as a man after all' – he thought – 'better for him.'

After the message finished, he picked up the telephone receiver and pushed a button that connected him with his operations center, located two stories below the penthouse. The center was one of three identical centers, one in Mexico City, another in Hong Kong, and a third one in Barcelona, Spain. The centers, filled with the most sophisticated computer and communications equipment, were the brains with which he monitored and controlled his far-flung empire throughout the world.

The voice of one of the 24-hour, year-round operators, answered immediately in a respectful tone, "Yes, sir."

"Get me Pancho in Houston, right away."

"Yes, sir."

He hung up and walked to a small cart that had several Baccarat crystal decanters. Taking a short lead crystal glass, he poured himself half a glass of Chivas Royal Salute, straight, with no water or ice, and swallowed almost one half of the liquid in one drink. He felt the warmth of the fiery whiskey going down his throat and a sense of relaxation started almost immediately. He had needed that drink all day long but could not afford to lower his guard during the important negotiations that had taken place throughout this Sunday.

The sensation of relaxation brought him, as it often happened, to the memories of his days in Havana, over thirty years before. He really missed those heady days more than he would admit it to himself.

He had arrived at Havana wounded and an exile, when he escaped from Mexico after the blood bath at the Tlatelolco Square during the last event of the student riots of 1968. He was only eighteen and had been a student in the National Autonomous University of Mexico. Young, impulsive and idealistic, he had been used as a pawn by the leaders of the so-called student movement. After the leaders disappeared, the Mexican Army massacred the students.

He had been able to save himself escaping with a friend to a small town in the outskirts of Mexico City where he had been treated by a country doctor who saved his life. Then, by bus to Merida in the Yucatan peninsula, and from there on a small boat to Cuba. Once in Havana, and after demonstrating to the satisfaction of the Cuban authorities that he was a bona fide communist, he was allowed to register officially into the National University of Havana as a political sciences student, which was what he had been in the University of Mexico. In reality, he was registered in a school that trained guerrilla fighters for the coming liberation wars in Latin America.

Much had changed since then. He was now immensely rich, extremely powerful and not a bit idealistic. Today, he was ruthless and ambitious, but the one desire that still burned in his heart was to make the United States pay for what he viewed as the toll of blood and suffering inflicted on the peoples of Latin America. And he was getting closer now.

He commanded a great army of loyalists who were willing to

go to almost any extreme for the handsome wages he paid them, provided that they could survive to enjoy the rewards. On the other hand, his prospective partners, with whom he had spent the day meeting and negotiating, could supply just what he did not have and no money in the world could buy: young men and women willing to make the final sacrifice of death if necessary for a cause.

The telephone rang.

He picked up the receiver and the operator said, "Pancho on line 3, boss."

"Thanks," he said, and punched the line 3 button.

"Pancho?"

"Yes, boss," responded a raspy voice.

"Our little plan to use your young gang members to give a good beating to that son-of-a-bitch."

"Yes boss, the guys are ready. I'm just waiting for 'operations' to tell me when he will be flying to Houston next and I'll give 'em the go ahead."

"We do not need to do it after all."

"No?" There was a little disappointment in the voice.

"Nope. The guy saw the light."

"Good boss, I'm glad to hear it."

"Thanks, Pancho, it's always nice to have you available, take care."

"I will, boss, bye," responded the raspy voice with a now satisfied tone.

They hung up and he swallowed the rest of the whisky. He then poured himself a new one and picking the telephone he punched a button that communicated him directly to one of the several apartments on the fifteenth and fourteenth floors of the building.

The nice-sounding voice of a young woman answered, "Hello?"

"Laurie?"

"Hi, darling, are you back?"

"I am."

"How did it go?"

"It went well," he answered. "Get your cute little ass in a small bikini and come up over to the swimming pool, I feel like exercising."

"I'll be up in a second. What kind of exercise did you have in mind?" she finished with a giggle.

1

ARREST IN HOUSTON

The MD-80 of Aeromexico's direct flight to Houston from Mexico City softly touched the runway at the Intercontinental Airport in Houston. In the first class section, Manuel Pardo-Gomez-Iglesias, known by family and friends as Manolo, verified the forms required of arriving passengers.

Mexicans use their mother's last name after their father's last name, something that has always complicated life for Americans who do not use their mother's maiden name as part of their name.

But Manolo had decided to use the composite name of Gomez-Iglesias as his mother's last name. He was simply Manuel Pardo-Gomez, but that name meant nothing while everybody in Mexico instantly recognized Gomez-Iglesias, the last name of his grandfather, the powerful banker, so Manolo had actually changed his name officially to Manual Pardo-Gomez-Iglesias

Manolo was used to crossing the international border between his country and the United States several times a year without any problems. Unlike thousands of his poor countrymen, there was always a red carpet to welcome people like him. He was neither nervous nor concerned when he put back the customs and immigration forms together with his Mexican passport in the inner pocket of his expensive silk sport jacket. After the door opened, he got up and walked out. He was tall. Almost 6 feet, slim and athletic, very good looking, with a Mediterranean complexion made slightly darker by his tan, that contrasted with his light brown hair and hazel-brown eyes. Always immaculately dressed.

Once in the D terminal of the Bush Intercontinental Airport, he walked through long corridors to Immigration. His passport was processed without a problem and he continued downstairs to the luggage pick-up areas. He had to wait a while until his two Louis Vuitton bags arrived. 'Wow, they are heavy,' he thought, when he picked them up and placed them on a little cart to walk to the Customs inspector. He was fully expecting to be asked to continue out of the area without being inspected, as always, but the officer asked him to go over to the inspection belts.

Manolo had not noticed it, but he had been closely followed from the moment he left the aircraft.

A little surprised at being asked to the inspection area, he walked there, placed the bags on the belt to be x-rayed and handed his declaration and passport to another officer who politely asked him to open his bags. Manolo complied with the request and observed while the officer searched.

The expert fingers of the officer started touching the lining of the bag he was examining. Manolo was very proud of his set of bags that had cost him a fortune, but, when the officer started touching the interior and the exterior of the bag Manolo noticed that there were four men standing around staring at him. He also noticed that the thickness of the sides of the bag was very noticeable.

The officer turned to look at him and stated softly: "I am going to have to cut the lining of the bag, there seems to be something hidden here."

"Something hidden?" said Manolo, "What?"

"That is exactly what I am about to find out," replied the officer, while he produced a Swiss army knife, opened it and started cutting the lining of his expensive Louis Vuitton.

Manolo was aghast at what he saw when the officer cut. A white powder started coming out by the cut and he immediately felt jerked to the ground as someone yelled, "Police, you're under arrest."

All the men who had been around him, were now all over him. One forced his hands to his back and handcuffed him, then pulled him up from the ground and started reading from a little yellow card: "You have the right to remain silent. If you speak, anything you say may and will be used against you in court. You have the right to have an attorney, and you have the right for your attorney to be present when we ask you any questions. If you cannot afford an attorney, one will be appointed for you. If you want to answer our questions now, you can still stop the questions at any time and consult with an attorney. These are your rights, do you understand them?"

Manolo, now in a state of mental chaos did not respond, so the man violently jerked him from the lapels yelling: "Do you understand?"

"Yes," said Manolo almost in tears while he then felt the warm trickle of his urine down his trousers. He did not have time to be embarrassed by it because he was being swiftly carried away. Around, other travelers looked surprised and amazed at what had just happened.

2

DON JOSE

On the top floor of the main building of the sprawling complex of the Bancomer Bank Central Office in a suburb of Mexico City, Jose Gomez Iglesias was sitting at the huge desk on the right side of his ballroom-sized office.

Don Jose, as everybody respectfully called him, was 80 years old, but had the appearance and physical condition of a man twenty years younger. His mane of silvery-white hair contrasted elegantly with the slightly dark skin that gave away the touch of Indian blood in his veins.

He had started very poor, at 16, working as a messenger for the same bank that he now owned. He progressed rapidly, thanks partly to his obvious intelligence, partly to his ruthlessness, and a good deal because of his marriage.

At 28, he had married Rosita, the former Rosa Maria Iribarren, a young socialite in Puebla, the large but provincial capital of the State of the same name in the Republic of Mexico. Nowadays everybody called her Doña Rosita. She was the key Don Jose needed to access wealth and power. Her father was a rich cattle and land-owner who managed to survive the revolution and agrarian reform with almost all his wealth untouched, thanks to his political connections.

Rosita's father was also the owner of a large chunk of shares of Banco de Comercio, S.A. (the name of which Don Jose, with a sharp public relations mind, changed eventually to Bancomer) and was instrumental in getting his son-in-law the strings necessary to rise like a meteor in the banking community to eventually become the largest shareholder of Bancomer, which in turn was one of the largest private banks in Mexico.

In 1982, Don Jose, as his father-in-law had done during the Revolution, managed to survive the nationalization of the banking industry without even a scratch, thanks to his fantastic connections. He was paid millions and millions of pesos for his interest in the bank. He exchanged them into U.S. dollars and Swiss francs before they devalued more and shrewdly invested in the United States and Europe.

Less than twelve years after having taken the banks, the Mexican government, now under a more enlightened administration, sold them back to the private sector. Don Jose bought back a controlling interest in his former bank and was now again virtually the owner of Bancomer.

"Don Jose, you have a call on line four from Mr. Thomas Moore, Laredo National Bank in Houston," said the voice of one of his secretaries through the intercom.

"I'll take it, Rosario," he responded and punched one of the many buttons of the large telephone console to the right of his English-style Lopez Morton desk. The console gave Don Jose one-touch access to every top executive in Bancomer all over the world. "Hi, Tommy, how is it going in Houston," Moore was the President of a Houston bank correspondent of Bancomer and the two had become good friends.

"Jose, I have bad news for you," the voice of his friend was unusually somber and the thoughts of Don Jose went immediately to his only grandson, Manolo, who had left for Houston the day before. He knew that the kid, as he lovingly called him in spite of being already thirty-two years old, was in love with every sport that involved speed and danger.

"What's wrong, Tom," he answered, feeling a steely grip in his belly.

"I just received a call from your grandson, Manolo," said Moore, "He has been arrested by U.S. Customs in the Intercontinental Airport. He stated that he could not make any long distance calls from the jail because his credit cards have all been taken from him, so he called me and asked me to call you, which of course I am doing immediately."

Don Jose could not help but feel relief that Manolo was not hurt, but at the same time was unable to understand what he had heard. "What do you mean arrested, why?"

"The charges are that he was trying to smuggle several kilos of cocaine into the United States."

"That is preposterous. They made a mistake."

"Yes, it must be a case of mistaken identity, but while the mistake is cleared, I believe you better get an attorney. The charges, as my legal department explains to me, are pretty damn serious. Do you want some names of local attorneys?"

"No," responded Don Jose, "I believe I know of someone who could represent Manolo. Just keep me posted of anything new that you find out, Tommy, and thank you."

"Don't mention it."

With a now somber face, Don Jose turned to the telephone console again and punched one of the buttons, which automatically connected him with Luis Gil, his Head of Security. Gil answered, "Yes sir?"

Don Jose just said "Luisito, can you come over to my office, asap?

"Sure, Don Jose."

"Listen, and bring with you that dossier on the attorney you checked for me in Houston."

"Will do, sir."

Luis Gil quickly got one of the thick files he had on a table next to his desk and climbed on foot the four stories from his office to where Don Jose's office was. One more way to keep fit.

A few minutes later there was a knock at the big double door of Don Jose's office. The two secretaries and Carlos, personal driver and bodyguard of Don Jose, knew that if Luis Gil said "Hello," and walked directly to the door to knock, it meant that he had been summoned by the chief.

"Come in Luisito," answered a voice from the inside.

From the sound of Don Jose's voice on the phone and the expression on his face now, Luis immediately knew that there was something not right. 'Probably some big lawsuit in Houston,' he thought. Don Jose, like almost every other business executive, hated being involved in lawsuits, which he considered just a waste of his time and money, particularly when somebody else filed them against him.

Luis Gil walked in and sat on one of the honey-colored wing chairs in front of Don Jose, who was punching another button to order fresh coffee brought in. He knew Luis was as much a coffee lover as he was.

Luis offered the thick file to Don Jose, who gestured with his hand for Luis to keep it. "Just make me a brief narrative of the man, Luisito, I already saw the file once. I'll go over it again at some later time."

Definitely the old man was not himself today. "Okay, Don Jose. You asked me a couple of months ago to check out this particular attorney for you because he had been very successful in a couple of cases against big Houston banks and because he is fully proficient in Spanish."

"That's right," remembered Don Jose.

"My investigation revealed that he was born in Mexico, the son of a prominent Mexican surgeon who died just a few years ago, and his American wife, who died over twenty years ago. Because of his mother, he had 'derivative' United States citizenship. Roberto chose his mother's American citizenship at eighteen, during the Vietnam War, and served in the armed forces of the United States."

"Yes, I remember that you mentioned that before," said Don Jose, adopting that child-like expression of curiosity that Luis Gil was so fond of.

Luis continued, "Duran, who already was a third degree-black belt in Karate and fluent in Spanish was recruited by the Special Forces Branch. It seems that the U.S. forces were having a lot of problems there with the crews of Spanish merchant ships that they used to supply advanced positions of the Army. Duran's commanding officer in the officer candidate's school, where Duran had been sent after an IQ test, referred him to Special Forces because of Duran's expertise in Spanish. Six months short of his nineteenth birthday, Duran was in Vietnam. He served a three-year stint participating in several highly secretive operations of which I could not get many details."

"Yes, I imagine that would not be very readily available," commented Don Jose.

"What is clear is that he distinguished himself enough to be promoted from second lieutenant to major in just three years, which is pretty extraordinary," continued Luis. "He was discharged having been highly decorated. Then, he came back to Mexico and enrolled in the School of Law of the National Autonomous University of Mexico at Mexico City. After graduating and getting his license, he opened a law office with a couple of fellow law school graduates and for a time had a thriving practice in the labor-law area."

· · ·

"All attorneys thrive in labor law in Mexico, off the hides of the private sector companies," said Don Jose with a sigh.

Luis smiled and continued, "Later, Duran's father asked his son to help him with a troubled small pharmaceutical firm in which he owned a 10% interest. Duran entered the company as a legal consultant. A Dr. Galvan, who was the president of the company, tried to block Roberto from any information on the business, but Roberto, ruthlessly and efficiently, managed to outsmart Galvan's clique and, in a coup-like movement, took over the board of directors and fired Galvan and his followers without paying one penny."

"That is quite a feat, I have never fired any employee that has not cost me a fortune," said Don Jose.

"Galvan had worked for the company during five years, the severance pay could have amounted to about a year's salary, yet Duran fired him and successfully defended the company in the lawsuit that ensued."

"I love that part," said Don Jose.

Luis knew why, it was Don Jose's own style. "With the coup, Roberto Duran became the president of the company. A couple of years later, purchasing from his own father and from some other shareholders, he had the control of the company that in time he turned into a medium-sized concern in the pharmaceutical field in Mexico."

"I seem to remember the company, they were our clients, right?" asked Don Jose.

"Yes they were," responded Luis before continuing, "By that time, Duran had started dating a very beautiful girl who worked for another bank as a public relations consultant and was very successful on her own. The girl decided to participate in a beauty pageant. She won the preliminary contest and became Miss Mexico City and then third place in the national contest. Later she married Roberto Duran and the couple became fashionable in the cosmopolitan and sophisticated circles of Mexico City."

"Yes, I remember the pictures at the Camino Real Hotel, very pretty girl. Good investigative work, Luisito."

"Thank you, sir. Roberto later sold his interest in the firm to a European concern and moved with his family to Houston, where he lost all his money in highly leveraged real estate investments at the time when the market in Houston was dropping like a piano trying to fly."

Don Jose gave a short laugh at the analogy of Luis. "And he lost all the money he had made in Mexico. Foolish."

"That's right," responded Luis. "He then had to work as an interpreter to support his family. First for attorneys and firms, later he got some kind of certification and worked for the federal courts."

"How did he come to get a license in the United States? Is it possible for a Mexican attorney to get a license up there?" Don Jose was as curious as always.

"Duran had to go to Law School all over again."

"All over again?"

"Yes, sir," responded Luis. "He was not a brilliant student, but passed the bar on the first try."

"It figures that he would not be brilliant, he had to work full-time to support a family. I understand that his wife is a homemaker."

"Yes, sir. Although she did some work before Duran was able to get work as an interpreter. The family survived on her work and the sale of their many heirlooms for about two years," said Luis.

"Yes, I remember reading about his wife, amazing woman," said Don Jose.

"Roberto then left the Court and opened his own law office. Interestingly, he has never lost a trial. Of course, he bargains most of the cases."

"What do you mean by that?" asked Don Jose.

"It is when a defendant pleads guilty without going to trial, after negotiations with the prosecutor to get a reduced sentence in exchange to saving them the effort of having to prove the charges in a trial," said Luis, "But it's still an impressive track-record."

"Good, I believe Duran is just what we need," said Don Jose, almost to himself.

Luis did not fully understand, but Don Jose was already leaning over to the telephone console and ordering, "Rosario, get me a call to Houston, Texas, the office of Roberto Duran. What's the number Luisito?

3

A CALL FROM MEXICO CITY

In the area of spectators in courtroom 700 of the federal court building in Houston, Roberto Duran was waiting for the detention hearing of one of his clients, the court- appointed case of a poor Spanish-speaking illegal alien who needed a defense attorney. Roberto's schedule hardly allowed him to take court appointments any more, but all the Houston magistrate-judges knew that Roberto never said no if the case merited it.

This case was typical. His client was an illegal immigrant who had been working in Houston for about three years and was making good money as a restaurant waiter. The man decided to go visit his relatives in Mexico. To be able to do that and come back into the U.S. without paying a 'coyote' an exorbitant fee for smuggling him in, he decided to buy a fake 'green card,' as the legal resident alien cards are popularly known. Unfortunately, he got a referral to a group of counterfeiters who were under the surveillance of 'ICE' as the new Immigration and Customs Enforcement Service is popularly known. As soon as he bought his card, he was arrested. Normally, the 'Migra' would have charged him with illegal entry, a misdemeanor, and sent him back to Mexico on a voluntary departure. His bad luck was that he was arrested with two more sets of green cards and social security cards that a couple of his co-workers had decided to buy also. The INS officer in charge of the investigation believed he was trafficking with the documents and charged him with a felony instead.

Roberto had met with his client the day before to tell him that the magistrate-judge would deny bail because he was undocumented and had no strong ties in the community and that it would probably be a good idea to work out a plea agreement with the U.S. Attorney to plead guilty to possession of counterfeit documents. Although Roberto felt that they could probably get off the hook with 'time served,' he would be deported from the country because it was still a felony. After being deported if he were to come back, he would be prosecuted for illegal re-entry after deportation and could face up to several years in jail.

When told the perspective, his client decided to follow Roberto's suggestion and go to trial on the case. Since he was charged with selling and distributing fake documents, Roberto felt that if he could convince the jury that his client was only a buyer of documents and not a dealer of them, he could be found 'not guilty.' It was worth a try. Of course that was down the road, the trial would be scheduled for maybe a month later. Right now Roberto would go through the motions of a detention hearing, although he knew, and had warned his client, that more likely than not, he would remain in jail until the trial.

Suddenly, his cell phone vibrated. He answered while walking out of the courtroom. It was Ginny, the receptionist of his law office who said, "Mr. Duran you have a phone call from Mexico City, the gentleman calling said to tell you that he is Jose Gomez-Iglesias."

Roberto was surprised. Like most people who have lived in Mexico, Roberto immediately recognized the name of the powerful owner of Bancomer.

"Is he waiting on the telephone?" he asked Ginny.

"Yes sir. He said it did not matter if it took long, he said he was going to wait," said Ginny.

"Okay," said Roberto, "Patch him through."

"Yes sir."

Roberto heard a couple of clicks and said in Spanish, "Hello, hello?"

A voice in Spanish at the other end of the line said "Counselor Duran, this is Jose Gomez-Iglesias, I imagine you have heard of me, otherwise you would not be on the line."

"Of course I have heard of you Don Jose," replied Roberto using the preface common in romance languages when you are addressing an older man or someone to whom respect is owed. "I don't think there's anybody in Mexico who hasn't."

"I don't know if that should be taken as a compliment counselor, but thank you for answering my call. The reason I insisted is because I have a matter of the greatest urgency to me and I need to retain your services, if possible."

Roberto wondered, his practice was mainly suing banks so, before he responded, he quickly made a mental review to try and remember if any of the banks he was suing was owned by Bancomer. He could not think of any, so he just answered, "I don't believe there would be any problem."

"I need to speak in person with you, if you are available," said Don Jose.

"Sure, but I thought you were in Mexico City."

"I am. I'm calling you from my office, and I want to ask you to .travel to Mexico City, tomorrow if at all possible. Your fee will be promptly paid. If you so desire, at your arrival here I will have a cashier's check in the amount of your consultation fee, and of course, all expenses will be taken care of."

"No problem Don Jose. I'll call my travel agent and book a flight and make arrangements and will call you back in a couple of hours. No need to worry about my fee, I'll send you my bill afterwards."

"You don't have to make any arrangements, everything will be ready," answered Don Jose with mild exasperation, like what you expect of someone talking to a young child, which reminded Roberto a little of the tone his father had frequently used with him. "My secretary will contact your secretary with all the details. The ticket will be first class of course. Also, you will probably have to spend the night here. Can you do it?"

"Sure," replied Roberto. If Don Jose was willing to pay for sixteen hours of his time at $300 an hour, he had no problem.

"Fine then, I will be only too happy for you to stay at my house, we have several guest rooms, but if you prefer a hotel…"

Roberto definitively preferred a hotel and anyway the offer was just part of the good manners observed in Latin countries, Don Jose was not really expecting him to accept. "Yes, if you don't mind Don Jose, I would prefer a hotel in order not to bother you or your family."

"You would not bother, but I understand. Which particular hotel, the Camino Real?"

"Exactly, the Camino Real is my favorite."

"I figured it would be," said Don Jose. "We will also make a reservation for you there. A car will pick you up at the airport and take you to the hotel."

Roberto wondered about the comment. Of course, the Camino Real was one of the very best in Mexico City. He just responded: "Well then that's it. When are we going to meet?"

"As soon as you have had a chance to freshen up, my personal driver will fetch you up at the Camino Real."

"Right, Don Jose, I am looking forward to seeing you tomorrow then."

"Yes, and thank you very much counselor."

After the call Roberto returned to the courtroom where his case was called shortly afterwards. Just as he had expected, his client was denied bond.

Don Jose hung up with Roberto Duran and turned to Luis Gil who was sitting in front of him.

"As you have heard, we are going to need the services of Mr. Duran."

"Yes, sir, I heard it, but why?" replied Luis.

"I just received a call from a banker friend in Houston. Manolo was arrested yesterday at the Houston airport. They are saying he smuggled cocaine."

Luis' mouth dropped. "What? That is crazy."

"I know, but my banker friend says the charges are very serious and we better get us an attorney."

"I guess so."

"Is there any way to find out from our end what happened at the airport in Houston?" asked Don Jose.

"Let me try, sir. I will get in touch with my contacts at the D.E.A. and report back to you."

"Do that, Luisito. And remember, I am terribly anxious."

"I understand, sir. I'll keep you posted."

Shortly before 5 p.m. that same day, Luis Gil came back to Don Jose's office.

As soon as he walked through the big double door, Don Jose got up from behind his desk and came to him.

"Well, Luisito, do you have something for me?" he said.

"I think I do, sir. First, my contacts at the D.E.A. in Houston have confirmed that U.S. Customs found cocaine secreted in the bags of Manolo."

Don Jose just shook his head with disbelief. "I just cannot believe this."

"Well sir, I have a hint. Remember that girl Manolo was dating and seemed so serious about?"

Don Jose responded "Sure, that beautiful blond. Julieta was her name," he said, "Something must have happened between the two of them. Manolo brought her home to introduce her to all the family. We all liked her very much, but afterwards he just didn't mention her again. I did not want to ask why. That's his business."

"Yes, sir." Luis knew that Don Jose was very respectful of the private life of others, to the point of seeming uncaring, although Luis knew well that he cared very much for those around him.

"Well," continued Luis, "Doña Rosita was a little concerned when Manolo brought her to dinner. She called me and asked me to do some questioning around and find out who she was."

"Typical female," smiled Don Jose, who cherished his wife.

"Typical grandmother," replied Luis. "So, I investigated a bit and found out that the girl's mother seemed to be the widow of a college professor who was killed before Julieta was born. She never remarried, so the child had to be the product of some extramarital affair. The mother is a professional accountant and very successful. She is a partner at a medium sized firm whose main partner is her father in law."

"You mean the father of the dead husband?"

"Right."

"He doesn't disapprove of his daughter in law having sex with another man?" Replied Don Jose, revealing his puritanical streak.

"I guess he looks at it pragmatically. The woman is relatively young and very beautiful."

"She must be, if she looks anything like her daughter. That young girl is ravaging," said Don Jose admiringly.

"Was," said Luis, laconically.

"What do you mean?"

"She committed suicide little over a month ago, she was pregnant when she died."

"Oh, my God," said Don Jose, realizing that the baby of the dead girl would have been, more than likely, his great-grandchild. Luis could see his eyes becoming wet.

"What do you know about Julieta's father?" he asked, instinctively knowing that Manolo's arrest had to be connected with the death of the girl.

"It is rumored that the father of Julieta is a powerful drug lord."

4

INTERVIEW IN MEXICO CITY

The following morning, a good three hours before the flight, as was his habit, Roberto drove his shinning gray BMW Z4 M Roadster to the Intercontinental Airport. At the terminal, the gate agent gave him his boarding pass and checked his luggage. Roberto hated carrying bags into the airplanes even if flying first class. Airplanes are always crowded nowadays. He then proceeded to the President's lounge because he had, as usual when he traveled, almost two hours to kill and he wanted to do some law research in his MacBook.

Afterwards, Roberto boarded the Boeing 737 for an uneventful but comfortable flight to Mexico City's Benito Juarez International Airport.

When Roberto got off the plane, a rush of memories came back to him at the familiar sights and odors of Mexico City's International Airport.

After going through immigration and customs, Roberto walked out to the airport lobby and saw a man holding a cardboard that said "Roberto Duran." He identified himself and the man guided him to a Mercury Marquis that had tourist license plates on it. Roberto wondered why Don Jose had said that his car would pick him up. This was obviously not his car, but then Roberto remembered that Don Jose had said 'someone will pick you up at the airport.' Soon after they were traveling to the Camino Real. The traffic was as heavy as he remembered it. When the car drove into the covered portal of the main entrance to the Camino Real, memories again rushed back to Roberto while he remembered his escapades with Lulu, now his wife of many years, while they were still dating and she participated in the Miss Mexico beauty pageant that was held in the Camino Real that year.

After giving a generous tip to the driver, he walked into the hotel's front desk to ask for the room that was supposed to be reserved for him. After checking into the computer terminal, the clerk said: "Actually Mr. Duran, you have a suite reserved for you."

'Don Jose really knows how to treat his attorney, Continental first class, a suite in the Camino Real, I'm going to enjoy this case.' - he thought.

The clerk handed Roberto the papers, already prepared before his arrival, just to sign his name. Then gave him a plastic entry card and called the bellboy. Roberto took the card, missing the old heavy metal key-chain with a beautiful golden square that had the hotel's logo.

At the suite, the sybarite in Roberto smiled approvingly at the rooms. He turned and tipped the bellboy after ordering a carafe of coffee. Mexican coffee is among the best in the world.

When the coffee came, Roberto poured out a cup and taking out his black Dunhill cigarette case with his left hand, and his black Dupont Chinese-lacquer lighter with his right hand, he lit a menthol light cigarette. Don Jose had said that he would have some time to freshen up, before his car picked him up so it was just a matter of waiting. Roberto sat on the big couch looking at the soft tans and browns of the elegantly appointed living room, wondering how much it would cost, 'who cares, I'm not paying for it' – he thought –.

About 20 minutes later, while Roberto was finishing his second cup of coffee immersed in proofreading some pleadings that his office would file the following week, there was a soft knock at the door. Roberto took-off his reading glasses, got up and opened. Standing in the hallway, were two men that looked fit and extremely well able to take care of themselves. 'Probably bodyguards' –thought Roberto.

"Counselor Roberto Duran?" asked one of them in a respectful tone.

"Yes," replied Roberto.

"Don Jose gave us instructions to bring you over to his office, counselor," replied the man.

"Fine, just let me get my briefcase. Would you care to come in?"

"No, thank you sir, we will wait for you in the terrace, over there," he answered.

"I will not be long," said Roberto, closing the door. He quickly picked up his papers, put them in the elegant light-brown Hartman briefcase where his Mac was, and walked out of the room to meet the two men who were in the terrace looking down with an uninterested gaze.

They all went down and to the front porch of the hotel. Parked in the middle, was a brand-new black Lexus LS450. The two men went directly to it and Roberto followed. One of them opened the right rear door and made a respectful motion for Roberto to get in.

Just the moment he was getting in, Roberto caught a glimpse of a 1977 black Chevrolet Caprice four doors. It attracted his attention because in 1977 he had bought a car exactly like it. Back then, it was one of the most expensive cars you could buy in Mexico because of import restrictions, today the old car seemed out of place among all the other luxurious cars on the driveway of the Camino Real.

The black Lexus drove off the hotel and into the 'Periférico,' a loop planned as a freeway but with so much traffic that it has almost turned into a normal street, just without the traffic lights. There are even vendors that approach the cars while they are stopped in the heavy traffic. Roberto smiled to himself when he thought that no one in Houston would believe that there are jaywalking vendors on the freeways of Mexico City.

Exiting the loop, the elegant car drove into the Colonia del Valle where Roberto had lived before moving to Houston. When the car finally reached the Bancomer Center, in the outer edges of the del Valle subdivision, Roberto was duly impressed. This was totally 21st Century. The ultra modern buildings were all interconnected by skywalks. Quite a feat for Mexico City, where the threat of earthquakes is ever present.

The car stopped at a central building. The men on the front seat got out, opened the door for Roberto, and led him into a pink-marbled lobby all the way into an elevator in the rear, obviously reserved for VIPs. One of the men produced a key and turned the lock to the eighth floor. The elevator went up directly into a luxurious waiting area where two very good-looking young secretaries smiled at Roberto while the men guided him into a double door and knocked. From the inside came the voice, "Come in."

When Roberto Duran walked in, Don Jose was a bit surprised. Duran seemed taller than the 5'10" that his dossier indicated. Also, he looked heavier than in his pictures and there were several threads of silver in the temples that indicated that he was not young any more. When they first spoke about Duran some time before, Luis Gil had pointed out that Duran looked a lot like the movie actor, Gene Hackman. Don Jose could not help but think that in person now Roberto looked very much like Hackman in that movie 'The Firm,' where Hackman played the role of a an attorney.

Don Jose could see that Duran was dressed in a kind of understated but very evident elegance. The gray silver silk suit, the elegant tie and the handkerchief that came out from the front pocket of the coat, all matched flawlessly. Luis had also pointed that it seemed to be a trademark of Roberto to always wear a matching handkerchief in the front pocket of his jacket.

Duran's mouth was smiling broadly when he approached Don Jose with a cordial, "It is a great pleasure, Don Jose." His eyes, as Don Jose observed, where more alert than smiling.

"Counselor, my pleasure to meet you in person," answered Don Jose, while walking from behind the enormous desk and guiding Roberto into the seating area at the center of the enormous private office. "Please, take a seat. May I offer you something, a cup of coffee, perhaps a drink?"

"Coffee will do, thank you," replied Roberto Duran while he sat on the button sofa to the left of where Don Jose sat.

Don Jose got on the phone next to him and gave some orders. Shortly after, one of the secretaries and a man dressed as a butler walked in and placed a silver samovar of aromatic coffee and a tea set of English Wedgewood porcelain in front of Don Jose, who served the cups himself.

While the girl and the butler moved around them, the conversation was reduced to small talk with Don Jose asking Roberto about his trip and if the accommodations that had been secured for him where of his liking. Roberto answered much in the same manner, commenting on how impressive Bancomer Center was.

It was the type of pleasantries that you are expected to engage in when visiting someone in Mexico. Don Jose was pleased with his guest's comments but did not show it, as is usually done among educated Mexicans.

When everybody left, Don Jose turned to Roberto and said very seriously: "Well counselor, you must be asking why I needed you to come, specially why all this rush and desire to speak in person with you."

"Yes, sir, I have."

"Very simply counselor, I, or rather my family... we are in a big mess," said Don Jose

5

SPOILED CHILD

Manolo was the child of Bertha, the only child of Don Jose. She had married very young, "You know counselor, the folly of extreme youth," commented sadly Don Jose, who apparently had disapproved of the wedding. The marriage had been a good and stable one, though. Bertha's husband had refused to work for Don Jose in the Bank. Instead he went back to the University and got a degree in engineering. Working hard and with much perseverance he had managed to give Bertha a pretty good life without accepting any help from Don Jose. Don Jose obviously felt respect for his son-in-law.

Unfortunately, he had died very young of a heart attack, when Manolo was only three. Don Jose had stepped in and virtually became Manolo's father. Bertha, who had been very much in love with her husband and was even today still mourning his loss, did not put up any resistance. She submissively reverted to her former status as daughter of Don Jose and quickly became more of a sister to Manolo than a mother.

Don Jose, of course, had spoiled the kid. Like most Latinos, Don Jose had wanted to have a son. When Rosita could not have any children after Bertha, Don Jose had been terribly frustrated.

Now, in Manolo he emptied all those desires of having a son to share the things he liked to do. Manolo seemed the ideal son, good natured, talented and studious. He enjoyed golf and hunting just as much as Don Jose did.

Unfortunately, even the best child may be badly spoiled by too much love and attention. By seventeen, Manolo gave the first indication of problems, but his grandfather was able to get him out of trouble with his power and money.

At eighteen, Manolo started racing cars and soon all his family was terrorized by the idea that he might be killed in a car wreck. Then he started doing all kinds of dangerous things. If anything was risky, Manolo loved doing it, parachuting, racing motorcycles, scuba diving, flying, anything, if it involved danger. But at least he had continued attending school and graduated from Universidad Iberoamericana, one of the most prestigious universities in Mexico City, with a degree in engineering, probably as a tribute to his father.

After graduating, Manolo seemed to settle down a bit and started a landscaping business. With the good connections of granddad, he got some juicy government contracts and the business thrived. Using the contracts as a springboard, Manolo set up a lucrative private clientele, very selected and exclusive. Soon, Manolo had a nice business with all the rich ladies in Mexico City who wanted a yard landscaped. The business had grown into commercial real estate as well and Manolo had become wealthy on his own.

Roberto was surprised at learning these facts. It really did not fit the profile of a drug trafficker at all, unless you wanted to believe that Manolo had done it just for fun. Roberto started believing that maybe he had another winner. He did have a striking record, but the reason was simple. He always tried to avoid the trial of cases that could not be won. He had the philosophy that a defendant is better-off pleading guilty with a good plea bargain than going to trial when the odds are heavily against him.

"Don Jose," started Roberto after the old gentleman finished his narrative of Manolo's background as Roberto had asked him to do when told of the arrest in Houston, "You need to understand a couple of things if I am going to undertake the representation of your grandson."

"Yes?"

"My client is Manolo, not you, although I imagine that you will be paying me, right?"

"Absolutely, I am ready to pay you this very moment," responded Don Jose, leaning over to look among some papers in front of him and producing a big checkbook.

"We'll get to that Don Jose, but right now I just want you to understand that Manolo is the client and what he wants to do and how he wants to handle the case is what I am going to do, not what you may instruct me to do. Do you understand?"

"I believe I do."

"Another thing is that you have to understand that nowadays it is extremely difficult for a foreigner in the United States to make bond if accused of drug-dealing. The anti-drug laws establish a legal presumption that a drug defendant is always a risk of flight and a danger to the community."

"Manolo is no danger to anybody. He may be a danger to himself, but not to others," argued Don Jose.

"I understand," said Roberto, smiling at the comment, "but we will have the burden of proving that he is not a risk at a hearing. To prove it, I will need much help from you."

"Counselor, you can have all my money and use all my power. Just get him out. Jail is no place for my grandson."

"I agree, but you must understand how difficult it may be to get him out. I do not want you to build high hopes, because I may be unable to do it. It may be that Manolo will stay in jail until the trial is over." Roberto could see that he was hurting the old gentleman, but he continued, "And he may remain in jail until we win the case, *if* we win the case," said Roberto, emphasizing the 'if.'

Don Jose's face was somber, but he was an intelligent and practical man. He did not dwell on negatives, never had. He just responded curtly, "I understand, just do your best."

"I will. Now, about my fee, I normally concentrate on just one big case at a time, so I'm really expensive--"

"Don't worry about that, counselor, just tell me how much you are going to charge and how do you want to be paid."

"I charge $300 dollars an hour, plus all expenses, including the time of my associates, paralegals and investigators and I require a retainer of $100,000 dollars which will be deposited into my trust account and disbursed as the case progresses."

Don Jose did not say a word, he simply took the big checkbook, wrote a check for $100,000 dollars and handed it over to Roberto saying, "It's drawn on a Houston bank, you should not have any problems cashing it."

Then, standing up, he said, "It is almost 3 o'clock, I would have wanted to have lunch with you, but have a prior engagement. I believe that your time will be better spent if you have lunch with our Chief of Security, Commander Luis Gil. He will tell you what we have been able to find out so far."

"Sure, it will be my pleasure."

"My driver and assistant will take you to the San Angel Inn where Luis Gil is supposed to meet you for lunch at 3:30, Luis will take you to the hotel after that," said Don Jose. "My car will pick you up at the Camino Real tomorrow for your flight."

"Thank you, Don Jose."

They shook hands and at the door of the office, before Don Jose opened the double door to his waiting room, Roberto asked,

"Why did you want me to come in person, we could have arranged all this on the telephone?"

"My friend, I understand that you lived in Mexico for a long time, is that right?"

"Yes, sir."

"Well then just let me say that you've been away from Mexico for too long."

Roberto smiled, remembering that in Mexico it is common knowledge that the government always keeps a tap on the telephones of powerful individuals. He just said, "I understand," while thinking how close to that we got in the United States with the Bush administration.

"Of course counselor, please keep me posted about everything," said Don Jose before Roberto left.

"I will."

The Lexus dropped Roberto off at the entrance to the San Angel Inn. The man seated next to the driver got out and opened Roberto's door. While he was exiting the car, Roberto saw again a black 1977 Caprice. This time it was coming into the driveway of the restaurant and stopped a few spaces behind the Lexus. Roberto caught a glimpse of several persons inside it but he could not be sure if it was the same car he had seen at the Camino Real before.

He thanked the two men and walked into the restaurant. The San Angel Inn was Roberto's favorite eatery in Mexico City, so Roberto was looking forward to the food and also to meeting Don Jose's top security man.

After advising the maitre that he was looking for a Mr. Luis Gil, the man said, "Of course, Commander Gil. Follow me, sir," as he walked to a table in a preferential place of the main dining room.

Luis Gil was a bear of a man. 6'2" and huge, not fat, huge, with the chest of a wrestler. He had blondish brown hair, blue-eyes, roguish good-looks and was wearing a well-tailored navy blue double-breasted wool suit and burgundy tie, socks and shoes. He stood up when Roberto approached and extended his hand "You're Mr. Duran, right?"

Very shortly afterwards they were on a first name basis. They had exchanged a few comments on the quality of the place and other subjects and soon discovered that they had lots of things that both liked and disliked.

Roberto ordered Myers rum with coke, Luis, a vodka tonic, "Make sure it's Stolichnaya," he warned the waiter.

After the drinks, they had a marvelous dinner of Chateaubriand with Béarnaise sauce accompanied by a red Bordeaux wine and followed by a delicious chocolate dessert, coffee, brandy and a couple of the cigars from the restaurant's own special reserve. Luis Gil had a sharp sense of humor that made Roberto really enjoy being with him.

While they were sipping at their after-dinner drinks and smoking the cigars, Roberto said, "Don Jose said that you would tell me about what you have been able to find out."

"Yes, it is not much. I must tell you that this is just a theory."

"I understand."

"Manolo was dating a very beautiful girl whose name was Julieta Velasco."

"You used the past tense."

"Yes, the girl killed herself about a month ago by ingesting barbiturates and locking herself into her mother's house garage with her car's engine running."

"Oh my..."

"It gets worse. She was pregnant, presumably by Manolo."

"Her relatives, then?" asked Roberto.

"Her father, I believe. I suspect he may be a big time drug baron."

"Do you know who he is?"

"I have an idea of who he could be, but I am not sure if the man I am thinking of is really the father of Julieta," said Luis.

"How is it that you suspect the father of being a drug lord?" asked Roberto.

"Manolo kind of hinted at that after he stopped going out with the girl. He seemed to be genuinely interested on the girl but then he stopped seeing her altogether," responded Luis. "From an investigation that I carried out upon request from Doña Rosita, Don Jose's wife and the grandmother of Manolo, and from what Manolo had told me, I came to the conclusion that the father had to be a drug baron."

"What are you planning to do?" asked Roberto.

"I guess I will try to get in touch with that man and then go on from there."

By the time they finished their third brandy and their second cigar it was already evening, Luis drove Roberto back to the Camino Real in his car, a champagne-colored 1957 Thunderbird in mint condition.

Luis put the soft top down, the weather, as it is almost always in Mexico City, was tempered and the evening marvelous. The ride to the hotel brought them to pass by several of the wonderful sites of the City. The Angel, as the monument commemorating the independence of the country is popularly known, shone its gilded beauty illuminated by the big reflecting lights. Then, Chapultepec Park, in which the Castle residence of Maximiliano, the ill-fated, French-backed, emperor of Mexico during the time of the Civil War in the United States, could be seen atop of the hill called 'the crickets' which gave its name to Chapultepec Park. In Aztec, crickets are called 'chapulines' and hence the name of the park. The castle seemed a fairy tale apparition among the modern buildings of the sophisticated city.

Roberto, amazed at how beautiful Mexico City could be, was delighted by the ride and he exclaimed, "Praise the Lord oh my soul. Praise Jesus! Mexico can be really beautiful with this weather and your nice company."

When Luis had investigated Roberto, he had found out that Roberto was considered by many of his acquaintances as deeply religious, although Luis could not find to what church did Roberto belong. It had been strange, but not unheard of, that someone as tough as Roberto could be very religious, even mystical, but after meeting him and joking around in the restaurant it seemed strange because Roberto was so normal and down to earth. Luis decided to ask him.

"What religion are you, Roberto"

"None," responded Roberto, and then continued, "What I have is a personal relationship with my Lord and Savior, Jesus Christ."

Luis asked him to explain and when Roberto concluded his explanation about being a born-again Christian and how he considered that to be a relationship with a living God and not a religion at all, Luis just said, "Interesting."

Luis had said it casually, but the words of Roberto had made a strong impact in his mind. Luis would soon discover the truth about that relationship.

By that time, the Thunderbird, which had been driving on Reforma Avenue, reached Mariano Escobedo and Luis turned to go into the rounded driveway of the Camino Real hotel.

While he got out of the car at the Camino Real, Roberto once again noticed a black 1977 Caprice coming into the driveway. His years in Vietnam had given Roberto an instinct for danger that made a red light start blinking in his brain. Too many coincidences that he had seen what seemed to be that particular car three times that same day.

Roberto shook hands with Luis who had gotten out of the Thunderbird to say good-by and walked into the lobby. Then, after Luis had left, acting as if he had forgotten to tell his friend something, Roberto walked out to the car porch and, as if trying to catch the Thunderbird on the street, walked quickly by the Caprice, which was parked next to the sidewalk. There were four men inside. All of them seemed to be the kind you would not like to meet in a dark alley. Roberto, acting as if he had not been able to catch the other car, walked by the Caprice on the way back into the lobby. The four men never moved, but Roberto could feel their stare on the back of his head while he walked in.

Once in his suite, feeling sorry for not having his Smith & Wesson snub-nose .38 special airweight revolver, Roberto set up a series of small booby traps designed to make noises in case someone tried to break into his room.

Maybe he did not need to worry. Maybe the men were employees of Don Jose sent by him to keep a watch on his attorney. Powerful men are sometimes pretty strange. But Roberto believed Luis Gil would have told him about them, and in any case, he preferred to be safe rather than sorry.

———

But, nothing happened. The following morning Roberto got up, had his time of prayer, then down to the fitness room for his 40-minute daily routine of simulated karate combat/aerobic exercise, then back to his room to shave, take a bath and get dressed. Afterwards, he checked out. Don Jose's men were waiting for him in the black Lexus and they all left for the airport. The Caprice was nowhere to be seen and, in the sunlit beauty of Mexico City's late fall morning, Roberto thought that he was making too much out of nothing.

6

THE DETENTION HEARING

The courtroom on the seventh floor of the Houston Federal Courthouse, was packed with the usual assortment of characters that you would expect to find for the criminal docket call at 2:00 p.m.

Roberto sighed, it would be a long afternoon. He had visited with Manolo in jail a couple of days before, after returning from Mexico City, and they planned the strategy to follow after filing a short continuance of the hearing.

As part of the strategy, Roberto had his office contact the people who Don Jose had suggested and selected a group of four-teen whom he could call to testify at the detention hearing. It was important to impress the Judge with all the people who were willing to testify that they knew Manolo and/or his grandfather.

Roberto then visited with the Assistant U.S. Attorney in charge of the case, Bill Block. Roberto knew Block from his days as court interpreter and from working in several cases against him and he regarded Block as a tough but very fair guy. Block had been adamantly opposed to recommending bond for Manolo even though Pre-Trial Services –which prepares a background report on every defendant– had recommended a five million dollar bond, but Roberto was able to get Block to promise that he would not appeal the decision to the District Judge, should the Magistrate set a bond amount.

As usual, the short cases were taken first, so it was not until 3:15 that Manolo's case was called for a probable cause and detention hearing. Roberto and Block stood up and announced they were ready. As procedure required, the government would call its witnesses and Roberto would cross-examine them. After that, Roberto would try to prove that his client was a good bond risk by calling defense witnesses whom the government could cross-examine. Finally, the Magistrate-Judge would ask for arguments from both counsel and make a ruling. It was almost a mini-trial, only that without a jury.

Block called the name of an agent. The DEA agent called by the government as a witness was a junior rookie agent. It was normal when the government is dealing with a tough cross-examiner, and Roberto was considered very tough. Roberto was not surprised, it was part of the tricks that ordinarily go on in a courtroom. The purpose was preventing Roberto from being able to discover any valuable piece of evidence before the government was prepared to give it to him. After thirteen questions, Block said: "Pass the witness, your Honor."

"I have just a few questions, Your Honor," said Roberto.

"Go ahead," said the Magistrate-Judge.

"Agent Dunbar, as I understood, you are a D.E.A. agent but currently work with Customs agents in the High Intensity Drug Trafficking Area Task Force, generally known as HIDTA, is that correct?"

"Yes, sir. That's correct."

"How many of you participated in the actual arrest of my client?"

"I believe there were four of us."

"You are including the Customs agent who was also present?"

"No, I was just referring to the HIDTA agents."

"So that would make five law enforcement agents in all, right."

"Ah... er... if you count the Customs inspector as one, yes."

"Agent Dunbar, is it customary to have five officers always present when luggage is being inspected at the airport?"

"I... don't understand, your question."

"I mean, is it customary to have five officers ready to jump on a suspect while he is being inspected at the customs counter?" repeated Roberto.

"Objection, assumes facts not in evidence, Your Honor," said Block.

"Overruled, we don't have a jury to impress, gentlemen, please remember that," said the Magistrate, sounding as a school-teacher exasperated at her students.

"Please answer," said Roberto.

"Ahh... well... I'm still not sure... we were not ready to jump on him, the Customs inspector called us after he found the cocaine secreted in the... the--"

"What you are telling us is that it was not until after the inspector found the cocaine that you were called in. That you were not standing next to my client while he was being inspected?"

"Objection, Your Honor, multifarious, it's two questions in one," said Block.

"Overruled."

"Can you answer please? You were not standing next to my client while the inspector went over his bags?"

"No... no, we... I was not."

"Were other agents?"

"Ahh... ahh... no, they were not."

"You're sure?"

"Objection, the witness already answered, Your Honor."

"Overruled! Agent Dunbar, were there any agents standing

next to the defendant at the time of his inspection, yes or no?" asked the Magistrate turning to the witness.

"No ma'am, there were not," answered the witness with a shaky voice.

"Pass the witness, Your Honor," said Roberto.

'You're screwed!' –thought Roberto–. The man had perjured himself and it would be fairly simple to have his own fellow-officers, possibly other travelers as well, testify that the agents were all standing around Manolo at the time the inspector opened the bags and jumped on Manolo right after the cocaine was discovered.

Roberto knew that an inexperienced agent would make just such a mistake because, more than likely, he would have been advised by the Assistant U.S. Attorney before the hearing that the government did not want to divulge the fact that they had received an informant's tip on the cocaine that Manolo had in his luggage. So he set the trap and the man fell. Roberto was almost positive that an informant had been involved.

Block knew what had happened, but there was nothing he could do at the time, he just said with a sigh: "The government rests, Your Honor."

"Do you have any evidence you want to offer, Mr. Duran?"

"Yes, Your Honor, I have a few witnesses and I'll just proffer the testimony of most others who are here, to save time."

"Good, go ahead," said the Magistrate with a relieved expression, looking at the packed courtroom.

"I would like to invoke the rule, Your Honor," said Block.

Roberto obligingly complied by asking his witnesses to wait outside the courtroom until called in one by one and telling them not to discuss their testimony with each other. It was just a maneuver by Block to get even at Roberto and to bother him a little. It was of no consequence whatsoever.

"I call my client," said Roberto.

The Magistrate-Judge looked surprised. She knew that

Roberto was an experienced litigator, so she did not say anything, although she would have warned an inexperienced practitioner of the dangers of calling a defendant to testify at a detention hearing.

After asking Manolo to give his full name for the record, Roberto said, "I just have one more question, Mr. Pardo. Did you know there was cocaine in the bags when you were sent to the inspection area?"

"No sir, I did not know."

"Pass the witness, Your Honor," said Roberto.

Block, who had been as surprised as the Judge when Roberto called his client, pondered for a moment, then said, "Are you asking us to believe that you did not know that you had cocaine in your bags?"

"I did not know there was cocaine in those bags," responded Manolo firmly.

"You did not know there was cocaine in your bags when you checked them at the Mexico City airport?"

"There was no cocaine in the bags I checked in Mexico City."

"So the cocaine miraculously appeared once in Houston?" asked Block with an exaggerated ironical tone.

"I can only tell you that the bags I myself packed in Mexico and then documented for the flight, did not have anything hidden in them, someone had to change them before I got to Customs," responded Manolo, following Roberto's instructions to tell the truth but explain what he knew.

"I remind you sir that you are under oath," said Block, now with a menacing attitude.

"I know, and I swear to God that I did not know anything about the cocaine that was found there."

Block rolled up his eyes and said with a tone of disgust, "Pass the witness."

Roberto was proud of how Manolo had followed his instructions. He had been a little concerned about calling him. You can never know how someone is going to react in the witness stand and it is very easy for a guilty man to get entangled in his lies. But Roberto had come to believe that Manolo was really not guilty.

He called only four witnesses more. He had fourteen available, but did not want to tire the Magistrate with repetition. They were all prominent members of the community, one banker, one wealthy businessman, one doctor and one lawyer, who all testified that they knew Don Jose very closely, had been associated with him in one way or another, and were well acquainted with Manolo and the fact that he spent at least two months of every year in the United States. They all testified also that they had a very high opinion both of Don Jose and of Manolo.

Block briefly cross-examined every witness emphasizing for the Magistrate that they really had no control over Manolo. That if he were to be out on bond and decide to leave the country and not come back, there was nothing the witnesses could do about it. The last cross-examination question was the typical, "If you knew that Mr. Manuel Pardo was a drug trafficker, would your opinion of him change?" The question was foreseen by Roberto who advised the witnesses to, of course, answer with the truth. All of them had answered, "Yes, it would change."

After the cross of the last witness he had called, Roberto proffered the testimony of the others. It was basically the same testimony as those who testified.

Finally, the Magistrate called for arguments.

"Your Honor, the government's position is that the statutory presumptions have not been overcome by the defendant. Statute imposes on the defense the burden of showing that he would not be a risk of flight or a danger to our community. Even if we were to assume that Mr. Iglesias's ties to Houston are strong enough, and we do not think that to be the case, the danger to the community remains, as every drug trafficker is a danger per se. One of the factors that the Court may consider for your determination is the weight of the evidence. In this case the evidence is overwhelming," finished Block, and sat down.

Roberto stood up, "Your Honor, the evidence cannot be overwhelming when there is no evidence of knowledge whatsoever. Also, we still have a presumption of innocence in this country. By the way, my client's name is Mr. Pardo, not Mr. Iglesias, and we would like the record to reflect the name accurately. Mexicans use these long names because they want to show their connection to someone famous, but the last name is Pardo."

"I am sorry, *it is* Mr. Pardo," said Block.

Roberto continued, "We will prove that Mr. Pardo was a totally innocent victim of a trap set by a prominent Mexican drug trafficker to take revenge on him, that the trafficker advised the DEA, probably through an informant, of the cocaine that could be found in my client's baggage to trap him. Therefore, the presumption of innocence itself is sufficient to overcome the alleged danger to the community--"

"There is no evidence of what Mr. Duran is alleging, Your Honor," interrupted Block.

"My client testified that someone had to put the cocaine in his bags without his knowledge, Your Honor," responded Roberto

"Maybe Mr. Duran wants to take the witness stand," said Block, by now clearly upset.

"Is that part of your argument Mr. Block, or just a sidebar," said the Judge testily.

"I'm sorry Your Honor," responded Block.

"Go ahead, Mr. Duran," said the Judge

Roberto continued, "As to the issue of risk of flight, we have shown that Mr. Pardo has more than enough ties and interests in Houston and other places of this country to make it necessary for him to face these charges or be prevented from returning to a country where he spends long periods of time and where he transacts an important portion of his business. Furthermore, should my client disappear, his family in Mexico is so prominent that I do not believe he could avoid prosecution from his own government."

"Your Honor, it is precisely because his family is so prominent that the government fears Mr. Iglesias... I'm sorry, Mr. Pardo, will not appear. His prominence itself would prevent him from being touched down there." Just as he finished speaking, Block realized that he had fallen into another of Roberto's subtle traps. Roberto chuckled to think that now he had an admission by the government that Manolo's family was prominent in Mexico.

"Your Honor, being born in Mexico, I take offense at the comments of the prosecutor. Surely Mexico has a judicial system that can and will prosecute the crime," said Roberto, and noticing Block's contrite expression, he could not help but to smile.

Roberto continued, "The bond we are willing to accept is the Pre-Trial Services' recommendation of five million cash or surety. We are prepared to post the bond right this very moment, Your Honor."

"Anything more Mr. Block?"

"No, Your Honor, just that we don't believe that either presumption has been overcome."

Roberto's heart started beating faster, he knew that a District Judge, where the Magistrate's decision would have to be appealed if unfavorable, very seldom would release on bond a defendant who has been denied bail by the Magistrate.

Calmly, the Magistrate-Judge spoke, "The Court is ready to rule. As to the issue of probable cause, I do find there is probable cause to believe an offense was committed and that the defendant was the one who committed it. As to the government's motion to hold the defendant in custody until trial, I find with respect to risk of flight that the defendant has been able to establish sufficient connections with our country to make me conclude that there are conditions that will guarantee his appearance at trial. As for danger to the community, Mr. Duran is right, we still have the presumption of innocence, and it is incumbent upon the government to make an affirmative showing that, if released, a defendant will constitute a danger. It is not sufficient to say that drug trafficking is always a danger to the community. No showing has been made in this case that this particular defendant would engage in such activity if released. Therefore, I set a bond in the amount of five million dollars, cash or surety."

Roberto's stress dissipated. He looked at Manolo and could see that his eyes were watering.

The Magistrate then called Manolo in front of her and read the conditions aloud. One of them was that Manolo could not leave the country, so his passport, which had been taken by customs, would not be returned to him until the case was finished.

Getting up, but before leaving the courtroom, the Magistrate asked informally, "Are you going to post the bond right now, Roberto?"

"Yes, Judge."

"Fine, my clerk will swear your client to it and I'll see you both at his arraignment," she said and she left.

Roberto turned to Manolo, who was standing next to him and gave him a hug, "Congratulations guy."

"Thank you dearly Roberto," he said in Spanish, " I will never forget your help and be sure that I will not let you down, I'll stay here and face the charges."

"You better Manolo," responded Roberto, also in Spanish, "Otherwise your grandfather is going to be out of an awful lot of money, and I will be greatly embarrassed."

7

JULIETA

Walking into his office back from Manolo's detention hearing, Roberto said hello to Ginny sitting at the reception counter and went on to the office of Dana, his personal secretary, where he sneaked in and said: "Dana, can you come in a minute," and continued to his private office located in one of the two corners of the half-floor suite, where he sat at the Lopez Morton desk and said:

"The Pardo case, Dana. Get in touch with Cavazos" –who performed most of the investigative work for the law office– "And tell him that I need him to find two or three witnesses who were in the customs area of the Intercontinental Airport at the time the Aereomexico flight in which Manolo Pardo was arriving was cleared through customs. They have to be able to testify that they saw government agents jump on Manolo right after the cocaine was discovered in his bags. Of course, the usual requirements as to reputation and character of the witnesses. Also, get me Commander Luis Gil on the phone, and tell Connie to prepare a motion to suppress for the Pardo case, I know it won't fly, but let's give the government some trouble. Do I have any messages?" Dana gave him a stack of five. "Okay, thanks, is that it?"

"Yes Roberto, do you want me to get you Commander Gil first?"

"Yes, please Dana, I called Don Jose from my cell phone from the courthouse, but I need to tell Luis."

"Sure," said Dana, and left.

Roberto had called Luis on his arrival back to Houston to tell him about the four men in the black Caprice in the Camino Real, adding the comment that they might have been sent there by Don Jose. Luis had said that it was dubious that Don Jose would send them without the knowledge of Luis. Also, the men working for Don Jose did not fit the profile that Roberto gave him. Don Jose's men would be well-dressed and in a brand new car, not dressed in shabby clothes and driving an old car. Luis promised that he would investigate. Roberto wanted to tell Luis that Manolo was out and it was a good opportunity to know what had happened.

Shortly afterwards Dana called through the intercom, "Commander Gil on four, Roberto."

"Thanks Dana," said Roberto picking up the receiver.

"Hello, Luis, how are you doing?"

"Hi, Roberto, I heard that you called Don Jose with the good news that Manolo is out on bond."

"Right, we lucked-out and Manolo is free, for the time being at least."

"That's great news. What are you going to do next?" asked Luis.

"I asked him to meet with me tomorrow morning at 8:30 to start working on the facts of the case. I am planning to ask him about the girl right away."

"Do that. It will probably throw him off balance. I do not think it is something that he will be very eager to discuss," said Luis.

"I imagine," said Roberto.

"Now, about that mysterious Caprice," said Luis.

"What about it?"

"Bad news, as I suspected, the license plate number you gave me is of a car reported as stolen, but does not belong to the Caprice, which more than likely is also stolen. In short, the guys are untraceable, unless you can give me a more detailed description."

"Not really," said Roberto, "They were inside the car and I just walked-by. Anyway, if there is something fishy, we will probably find out soon."

———

The following day, at exactly 8:30, Ginny called on the intercom to say that Manolo was in the waiting room. Roberto asked her to send him in. Then, he stood up and walked to the door to greet him.

"Hi, Manolo," he said in Spanish when Manolo got there.

"Hello Roberto, I am all geared up to spend the whole day here with you," responded Manolo, probably hoping that Roberto would answer that it would not have to be all day.

"Be assured that we are going to spend the whole day today and as many more days as necessary," said Roberto, who could not help but feel amused at the annoyed expression of Manolo.

He then made Manolo sit on one of the wing chairs in front of his desk and he sat back on his swivel wing chair. He preferred to be at his desk to take notes as necessary. Ginny was just walking in carrying two cups of coffee in the beautiful white-with-a-gold-rim Noritake porcelain of the office. Manolo said "Thanks Ginny," while Roberto noticed the expression of adoration on Ginny's face.

After Ginny left, Roberto said, "Okay, how about this for openers, tell me all about a girl named Julieta." Roberto noticed that Manolo's reaction was immediate, his face became pale.

"How did you... well I imagine that my grandfather told you about her," said Manolo.

"Well, go ahead, tell me the whole story," said Roberto.

"Sure, but I can tell you right now, she has nothing at all to do with this mess," responded Manolo.

"Let me be the judge of that," responded Roberto.

It was in Mexico City, almost one year before.

Manolo was driving his fire red Porsche Carrera convertible with the top down in Polanco around the Nikko Hotel. This area is one of the most fashionable districts of Mexico City, an area of about ten blocks that contains some of the most expensive and exclusive boutiques, restaurants, bars and hotels, plus plenty of apartment buildings.

He was driving casually. It was a quarter-till-two and he had a lunch appointment with some friends at two o'clock. In Mexico City lunch time for the business and professional people begins at around two in the afternoon and continues until four-thirty or five. Manolo had arranged to meet three friends for lunch at the Bellinghausen, a marvelous German restaurant in the heart of the Pink Zone, which used to be as fashionable as this area but now houses too many skin businesses and has decayed.

One of the things Manolo enjoyed about his landscaping business was that it allowed him to roam the streets of the City at almost any time of the day, and he could arrange his schedule to suit whatever he wanted to do.

The red Porsche would attract attention anywhere in the world, but in Mexico City it meant that you were extremely wealthy. Importation taxes almost double the already expensive price tag of the car.

Manolo put the manual shift in neutral to let the car roll smoothly ahead by its own inertia while he looked over on to the sidewalks seeking attractive girls among the crowd of well-dressed and sophisticated-looking people. Like any Mexican who is single, rich and thirty-three years old, he had an unending string of affairs. Manolo, although he lived in his grandfather's mansion as was usual among young, unmarried Mexicans, kept a hideaway in a very discreet building on a very discreet street not more than four blocks away from where he was then driving. That was what most apartment buildings in this area were for, lunch appointments were always made hoping to be able to pick up a good-looking girl who, after a proper lunch, could probably be persuaded to visit 'my den' as most Mexicans call them.

Suddenly, Manolo could see a group of three girls walking nearby. Like it's usual in that place, several would-be suitors followed them trying to engage in a conversation that could begin a friendship. Manolo revved-up the engine to make the girls look at him, successfully it seemed, and then signaling to the driver behind him, double parked the car and turned off the engine amidst the angry honking of the same driver who totally ignored the signaling. Manolo, oblivious to the honking, jumped off the Porsche, responded to the other driver's verbal assault by giving him the finger and then approached the girls. The three of them were pretty, but the one in the middle was exceptional. Tall, at least 5'8", with sculptural body, very blond hair and enormous green eyes that were smiling at Manolo's display at the time. She was probably the prettiest girl he had ever seen. Manolo started the flirt by introducing himself and, as always, the three girls were properly impressed at the mention of his name.

Thirty minutes later, the Porsche now properly parked –valet parking of course– they were all seated in the rear terrace of the Bellinghausen. The girls had called a fourth friend and, with Manolo's friends, the eight were now prepared to have fun. Manolo had monopolized the blond girl.

Her name was Julieta Velasco. "Velasco what," had asked Manolo, the archetypical example of his name-conscious society,

"Just Velasco, it's my mother's name, my father left us when I was just a child," she had said naturally. Manolo was impressed by her simplicity, 'Maybe, just maybe,' –he had thought– 'I have found that black pearl we all dream about but very seldom find.'

She had said: "Okay, but I have to be back at the bank by four," when Manolo offered to buy them lunch. "No problem, I'll drive you myself," he said. "In your red Porsche," she had said smiling, but sarcastic. "Yes, in my red Porsche," had responded Manolo, blushing a little.

She was nineteen, worked for the bank owned by Manolo's grandfather, lived with her mother, and seemed to be 'nice'. Nice to Manolo meant that he would not get to sleep with her. Not right away, at least. But sleeping with her was not that important anymore, Manolo was falling in love.

The lunch was great. Food, as always in the Bellinghausen, was marvelous and the conversation, lively. Nevertheless, dutifully at a quarter-to-four, Manolo got up from the table and, calling their waiter, asked him to put the bill on his tab, he had to leave. They said good-bye to the rest of the gang. The other three girls and Manolo's friends would stay. On the way out, Manolo told the waiter to be sure to cut the bill at that very time. "These suckers have all intentions of getting drunk, let it be on their own, not on me." The waiter nodded knowingly.

Manolo gave the ticket to the parking attendant and when the Porsche came, he opened the door for Julieta to get in. 'How great to have a low sports car when a pretty girl wearing a miniskirt gets in,' –thought Manolo– 'the view is marvelous.'

When they got to the branch office where she worked, a few blocks away, Manolo double-parked again, ignored again the angry honking of the motorists behind him, and helped her out of the car, again enjoying every second of it.

He left the car there and grabbed her hand. She did not resist him, and they walked hand-in-hand to the glass double doors of the bank. Before going in, she turned to him and said: "This is where you leave." It was not a question, it was a statement. For a split second Manolo debated if he should press to go in with her, but decided against it.

"I want to see you again... soon," he said.

"I do too," she said very naturally.

"How about tonight?" asked Manolo.

"No, in the evenings I go to school, but I would say yes if you buy me lunch tomorrow," responded Julieta.

Manolo would not only buy her lunch, he would have bought her the Eiffel tower if it had been for sale. They agreed that he would pick her up at one-forty-five the following day and Manolo made a quick attempt to kiss her on the mouth, but she turned her face and he kissed her on the cheek.

It didn't matter, his heart was beating wildly when, without opening the door, he jumped into the Porsche, started the engine, and pulled out with a screeching of the Pirelli tires. If the red Porsche was not enough to attract the attention of people around him, his loud and unmelodious singing sure was.

8

ROMANCE

B y noon Roberto and Manolo were still in Roberto's office with the door closed, so Dana ordered a couple of ham and cheese sandwiches together with more coffee and two lemon bar desserts from a nearby deli and, discreetly at around 12:15, she knocked at the door and advised Roberto that there was food for both. Roberto thanked her and they both ate without taking a break in the narrative.

Manolo had started dating Julieta regularly almost immediately. At lunch the following day, Manolo volunteered to take her home after work, but she refused explaining that three days a week she attended classes in the National Autonomous University of Mexico, and besides, she drove her own car.

"What are you studying?" asked Manolo.

"I'm working on my MBA, but it's only my first year, it takes four attending part time," she said.

Manolo had assumed that she worked as a secretary, just out of High School, but soon he learned that she had finished college one year before and was an executive trainee for Bancomer.

That second day, when after lunch he took her to the office, he found a parking place and parked the Porsche before getting out. Not that he was beginning to be civilized, but Julieta had insinuated that she had been a little embarrassed at the comments of her co-workers who had seen the display the day before. Manolo parked the Porsche illegally in a 'no parking' zone, but at least it did not interrupt the traffic flow. Julieta said she would just get out by herself, but Manolo would not even hear of that, he got out, opened her door, helped her out and walked her over to the door, where, again, he kissed her on the cheek, and asked her out to lunch the following day. She smiled, hesitated a little bit while Manolo began to sweat, and then said: "I would love to, will you pick me up here again?"

They had first met on a Tuesday. Then, went out for lunch every day for the rest of the week. On Friday, shortly before leaving the restaurant for her work, he asked her: "What about doing something tomorrow?" He tried to sound cool, but was really anxious to hear her answer.

"Well, I have to study on Saturdays, because I have no chance during the week, but maybe for a short while, in the afternoon," said Julieta.

"How about going to a disco?" said Manolo.

"No, not at night. Maybe to the movies," she said.

The following day they went to the movies. Manolo had asked her for her home address. He already had her home phone, he had asked her when they first met, as a precautionary measure, just in case she stopped working for the bank all of a sudden, so he would not lose track of her. When she said her address, Manolo noticed that it was in the Colonia del Valle, an upper middle class section, and it was a house, there was no apartment number.

When he drove there Saturday, shortly before four-thirty, he found the number. It was a nice house, nothing overly pretentious, but still, it seemed elegant and in good taste. He got out and rang the bell at the gate to the gardens. The house, as most in Mexico City, was totally surrounded by a fence, this particular one was a forged-iron fence, and the garden, which also fully surrounded the house, seemed very well kept. Manolo was an expert, because of his business, in recognizing an expensive garden, and this one was expensive, with all the plants and landscaping. He rang the bell and a maid came to open. In Mexico City, most houses have maids, it is still one of the advantages of being a third world country, labor is still relatively cheap. Manolo had assumed from the fact that Julieta was working full time and that her mother had been abandoned by her father, that the finances of the family would be tight. But when he was invited in, he could see that the furnishings were elegant and in very good taste. The same maid showed him into the living room and asked him to take a seat while the 'señorita' came down. While walking in, he noticed that the garage had the door open. Inside he saw a white four-door late model Cadillac next to a red Mustang convertible. Both cars were very upper scale in Mexico. He knew that she was an only child, so he wondered if the Mustang was her personal car. He was wondering what Julieta's mother did for a living when Julieta came down the stairs. She was dressed in jeans and seemed younger than when in a formal dress. He had always seen her with her hair made up, but now she had it in a pony-tail and he could see that it was long and very pretty. This time it was Julieta who came to him and gave him a kiss on the cheek, and Manolo felt like a teenager with butterflies in his stomach.

They had a marvelous afternoon without the time constraints of her having to go back to work. After the movies they went to the Duca D'Este, a fashionable coffee shop in the now unfashionable Pink Zone. Manolo, who had been curious since they left the house, very cautiously began inquiring about what her mother did.

"She's a Public Accountant," said Julieta.

"Is she remarried?" asked Manolo.

"No, I guess she was very much in love with my father when

they splitted. It was just that, for some reason, she just could not live with him, but I really believe she is still very much in love with him."

"What's his name?" asked Manolo casually.

"I don't know," she said blushing a little, and then added, "Anyway, that's in the past, let's talk about something else."

———————

For the best part of four months it was almost the same routine. They would meet for lunch at least four days of the week, and then on Saturday afternoon they went to a movie theater, later to have a cup of coffee, and then back to Julieta's home. On the second of those Saturdays, Manolo met her mother. She was as strikingly beautiful as Julieta but with a complexion not as fair as Julieta's. Her hair was darker too, although her eyes were as big and as green as Julieta's.

The occasion was that she was pulling her white Cadillac out of the garage when they drove into the house. They had left the Porsche parked outside the house and gone out in Julieta's Mustang, as they sometimes did. They both got out of the car and Julieta introduced Manolo to her mother. She seemed very nice and asked Manolo to stay for a while, "But not too long, remember Carolina has the day off tomorrow and she has to go to bed early," she had said. The obvious implication was that she did not want the two of them to be alone in the house. Manolo assured her that he would be leaving in a minute and Julieta's mother said good-bye and left in her car. Obviously she was going to an elegant place because she was exquisitely dressed.

Manolo, who had a standing affair with a couple of other girls, found the routine marvelous. He would be with Julieta weekdays at lunch, then Saturday evenings, and then at night he would frequently meet with one of the other girls and have sex in his Polanco apartment. But, little by little he became more and more interested in Julieta. Their relationship had become closer. The kisses on the cheek had become kisses on the mouth and, sometimes when Julieta's mother was not at home, as she frequently went out to dinner on Saturdays, they would have a session of necking in the living room of her house. But Julieta, as a well brought-up girl, would never accept anything more than mere kissing and hugging. Manolo could feel that she was a very passionate girl, but she had great self-control.

As their relationship grew closer, Manolo became convinced that he wanted this girl. 'Being a virgin,' –he thought– 'I will probably have to marry her before I can get her.' But he was not at all scared about the prospect of marrying her. His mother and grandparents had often insinuated that he had to begin thinking about settling down, which to them meant marriage. So, Manolo began caressing the idea of marrying Julieta.

He brought her to his grandfather's home on a Saturday to meet his mother and grandparents and they all had a delicious dinner in the mansion. It was the first time her mother had authorized them to stay out later than ten-thirty, and when he drove Julieta home that night it was after one-thirty in the morning. When they got to her home and out of the Porsche, Julieta began looking for her keys to the outer gate but could not find them, so Manolo said: "Why don't you ring the bell."

She looked at him as if he were a strange animal and said, "Are you crazy, at this time Carolina is asleep, tomorrow is her day off."

"Oh, I see," replied Manolo, who could not see because he was accustomed to having servants around him in the mansion twenty four hours a day. She finally found the keys, opened the door and went in after a big and long kiss.

The following week, back to their routine, they were having

lunch in the Calesa de Londres restaurant. They had already eaten and were sipping at a cup of coffee when Manolo suddenly said: "Julieta, would you marry me?"

She almost dropped the cup and stared at him, "Are you serious?"

"Sure I am. Would you marry me?"

"Of course I would," she said, "you must already know that I love you."

"I love you too, and I think I would like to share my life with you," said Manolo, but then he added, "but of course, I believe we have to make love first, to see if we can really be a couple in every sense."

Her big green eyes were full of suspicion when she replied: "I don't think you have to make love to a boy to be sure you can get along."

"Nowadays, how can you be sure unless you try it," he said, "And besides, we are both modern, you should not be ashamed of being with me, I love you."

"I love you too, but if that is the way you want it, it will have to wait, I am not ready for that," she replied with finality, and added with a dry tone, "Let's go, I have to get back to the bank."

But it did not have to wait too long. Three weeks later they were having lunch in the La Mansion restaurant. They had exhausted all the restaurants in Polanco and the Pink Zone and were now trying this one on Insurgentes Avenue. The subject of marriage had not been mentioned again. It was shortly before Christmas and the weather was cold in spite of the sun shining. Because Manolo did not frequent La Mansion as much as other restaurants and because it had been full when they arrived, they were given a table outside. Julieta was complaining about the cold weather and Manolo said teasingly, "If you did not wear your skirts so short you would not be so cold."

She laughed and replied, "Don't complain, I've seen your eyes when I get in and out of your car and you love my miniskirts."

"Well, I don't love the miniskirts, but I do love to see you wearing them. But if you insist on wearing minis, why don't we go to Acapulco for a weekend, it's nice and warm over there," said Manolo just to tease her.

Julieta became pensive and then said, "If I were to say yes, this would be a good weekend to go, my mom is going to take a long weekend, she's traveling to the United States."

Manolo could not believe his ears and was not sure if she was only teasing him, but decided to press on with the subject. He said as naturally as he could: "Why don't you tell her that you are going to spend the weekend with some girlfriend and I will make a reservation in the Princess Hotel."

"No, the Princess is too big, the Pierre Marquez is much nicer and smaller, I was there once with my mom," said Julieta, and Manolo could not get even a hint of teasing in her voice.

"That's it then," said Manolo, "I will reserve the bridal suite in the Pierre Marquez arriving Friday night."

"We are not married, remember?" said Julieta. But at no time did she object.

"We'll take care of that as soon as we return," said Manolo, who added, "As a matter of fact, I will tell my mother and grand-parents tonight that I am planning to marry you."

"Will you tell them also that we are going to spend a honey-moon in the Pierre Marquez before getting married?" asked Julieta going back to her teasing tone.

"I don't think it's a good idea, they are kind of old fashioned," responded Manolo with the same teasing tone.

9

ACAPULCO

It was about 5:30 p.m. when Dana advised Roberto on the intercom that she was leaving. Roberto and Manolo had been talking all day long. Returning his attention to Manolo after Dana's call, Roberto asked: "Did you actually tell your folks that you were going to marry Julieta?"

"Well, I hinted at it, but I was really thinking of doing it," he replied.

"Even after spending a premarital honeymoon in Acapulco?"

"Yes, yes, that didn't matter," said Manolo, a little impatient and with great conviction. "It was what she told me while we were in Acapulco that changed everything."

That Friday afternoon, Manolo met Julieta at the private Bancomer hangar. Julieta had told her mother that she was going to spend the weekend with Ana Maria, one of her friends, in Cuernavaca. Ana Maria had been made part of the conspiracy and agreed to go to Cuernavaca by herself and call Julieta at the

Pierre Marquez in case her mother would look for her in Cuernavaca.

Manolo had ordered his own private Bonanza to be ready. It was a model B-35-V, with the classic V-tail, and Manolo was as proud of his airplane as he was of his Porsche.

A few minutes later they were airborne. Julieta, who had never flown in a small single engine airplane, was fascinated. Manolo was thrilled at her childish enthusiasm when they took off. Later, he allowed her to take the controls of the craft for a short while and promised he would teach her how to fly the Bonanza.

They got to Acapulco in little more than one hour. It was getting dark and Manolo flew over the bay so they could admire the magnificent horseshoe view of brilliant lights. They landed 15 minutes later and, after ordering the attendants at the Acapulco's Bancomer hangar to tie up the Bonanza, Manolo picked-up the rented Pontiac Firebird convertible he had reserved and they drove to the Pierre Marquez. Manolo had not been able to get the bridal suite on such short notice, but they got a beautiful big suite on the second floor of the two-story hotel, with a marvelous terrace and a breathtaking view of the ocean. The hotel is located south of Acapulco, outside of the fabled Acapulco Bay.

As soon as they got to the room, Julieta locked herself in the bathroom and changed into more formal clothes. It was already eight-thirty and Manolo had announced that he had made a reservation at Coyuca 22, one of the best restaurants in Acapulco. When Julieta came out of the bathroom, Manolo could not suppress an exclamation of admiration. He had always seen her in jeans or business clothing, even for an evening dinner at the Pedregal mansion of Manolo's grandparents, when she had been wearing a business type dress. This time she was dressed in a yellow silk dress. The dress bared all her back. She wasn't wearing any bra, which she did not need, her breasts were small, but firm and beautiful. Seeing all that fair silky skin, Manolo could hardly suppress his desire to make love to her right there and then.

Julieta was surprised too. She had always seen Manolo wearing a business suit and tie or a sports jacket on weekends. But now he was wearing white silk slacks, with matching white shoes and belt and an orange colored silk shirt with short sleeves that showed his tanned and muscular arms.

"How do you manage to get a tan, if you are always in a business suit?" she asked him.

"My little secret," answered Manolo, who had a tanning machine in his bedroom at the mansion, while they left the room to go out for dinner.

The Pierre Marquez and the Princess hotels are separated from the rest of the city by a mountain that climbs up to five hundred feet of almost vertical cliffs, known as Las Brisas. So, they got in the convertible and left the lush tropical gardens that surround the Pierre Marquez driving on the Costera Highway, following the coastline climbing up and up on the winding road until they got to the Las Brisas subdivision, where some of the best and most expensive residences of Acapulco are located. Unbelievable houses perched like eagle's nests on the mountainside. Don Jose owned one of the best houses there, but Manolo had decided to go to the hotel for obvious reasons. The list of owners of houses in Las Brisas reads like a who's who of the world. Hollywood and European stars and celebrities, Mexican politicians and millionaires, American executives, nobility from Europe.

Finally, they arrived at the Coyuca 22 restaurant, the name of which comes from the fact that it is located at number 22 on Coyuca street, also perched high on the cliffs surrounding Acapulco completely, but these to the north of the bay. The place is marvelous, the cuisine excellent, and the view of Acapulco Bay underneath your feet, unbelievable.

As usual, the maitre gave them one of the best tables, out in one of the terraces that overlook the bay. They walked holding hands to the table and Manolo felt proud seeing the envious looks of the male patrons of the place. They sat and Manolo looked at his Rolex King Midas. It was almost ten o'clock, still early for Acapulco, where the discos open at nine-thirty and the best time to be in them is between midnight and four in the morning. Manolo had a midnight reservation at Baby's. It was one of the most fashionable discotheques in Acapulco, and even with his name and his money he would be hard pressed to get a good table there without a reservation, so he wanted to be sure they would be on time.

They ordered drinks and, while they waited, they chatted pointing out interesting places of the view below them, or rather, Manolo chatted, because he noticed that Julieta had become a little uneasy. He asked her if there was something that bothered her, but she just replied that she was all right. The drinks came and Julieta swallowed her rum and coke.

Manolo, believing that she was nervous because of the perspective of making love for the first time, tried to ease her stress: "Calm down darling, there is nothing to worry about. If at any time you feel bad, just let me know, there is no rush."

She whispered more than said, "There are things that I need to tell you."

'Oh my,' –thought Manolo– 'Now I just need for her to tell me that her period has started.' Controlling his anxiety, he just said, "What's wrong darling," trying to put a note of reassurance in his voice.

"I have two things to tell you that are--" she stopped talking when the waiter came to bring some appetizers. After the waiter left, she continued "--Something that is very important to both."

"Go ahead, tell me, what's wrong."

"I do not know how important this may be for you, but for me it is important that we be honest with each other."

"Sure, my love."

"So, I have to tell you. You need to know who my father is."

"Is that really important, I mean, right now?" asked Manolo.

"Yes, yes, it is. It is very important for me that you know the truth."

"Fine, then tell me," said Manolo.

"My father is very powerful and very rich," she said, and Manolo thought for a moment that she was joking. Then he saw her eyes and knew that she was being dead serious.

"He is probably the most powerful drug lord in Mexico," she finished with a whisper.

Manolo was aghast. Here he was with the most beautiful girl you can imagine, someone with whom he had fallen in love and someone he believed to be a nice middle-class girl, and she was telling him that her father was a drug baron. But his shock was just beginning.

Julieta continued. "That is not the only thing you need to know. The second one is equally important for me," she said.

Manolo was already pretty unnerved, so he just said, "What is it?"

"You also need to know that I am not a virgin." She blurted it out.

Manolo felt like if a thunderbolt had hit him. The first revelation had left him very off balance, and now this. He had always considered himself a modern, open-minded man, but he had assumed that he was going to be the first man in Julieta's life. The 'macho' lurking beneath him jumped out and he felt a deep disappointment. He could only say in a hoarse voice, "How was it?"

She noticed the wide range of emotions going through Manolo and felt terrible. In an anguished voice she explained: "I was only sixteen and my mom sent me to a school in the United States for summer, to learn English. I was feeling terribly lonely.

The school was in Oklahoma City and nearby there was a military academy for boys. In one of the parties up there, when I was feeling the lowest, I met this Mexican boy. He was really nice and understanding and we both fell in love. He was also sixteen. Two months later we made love. We dated for a couple of months more. After that, I never saw him or heard from him again. I believe he stayed up there to continue his schooling in the United States." She jerked it all out like an avalanche, like wanting to get rid of a load as soon as possible.

Manolo was dumbfounded, but he slowly recovered. He ordered another round of rum and coke for both, then the wine and the dinner. By the end of their dinner they had both almost regained normality. Julieta, once having eased her conscience, had become again talkative and entertaining.

She was really in love with Manolo and had tried to be as honest and forthcoming as she knew how to be. She had no way of knowing that deep in Manolo was this hatred and fear of women whose conduct was 'light', a nice euphemism. Manolo was a womanizer, which was all right for him, but he expected a virgin for marriage. One of the features that had attracted him so much to Julieta was exactly the fact that she had made him respect her and would not allow him in their relationship to be anything else but a gentleman.

But now, deep in him there was a sensation of bitter disappointment that he just could not let go. The idea that there would always be another man that intimately knew his wife was something he would not accept. Julieta's revelation about her father provided him with the rationalization he needed to feel justified in getting out of the relationship. How could the grandson of the most important banker in Mexico think of marrying the daughter of a drug trafficker? No, no way. From that moment on, he could no longer think of marrying this girl. But, of course, he was not about to say anything.

After Coyuca 22, they went to Baby's. They got there almost at midnight. The atmosphere in the place was in exactly the right moment to have a lot of fun. They danced until around 3:30 a.m. Manolo, now that Julieta in his mind was just another broad, felt an urge for her body. Julieta, on the other hand, thought that Manolo had understood her and was now feeling desire out of love. They left the disco and drove back to the hotel. After they got to their suite, Manolo would not even wait for Julieta to undress, he just started caressing and kissing her. He then took off her dress, began kissing her beautiful breasts and made love to her passionately, almost frantically.

The next day they got up late, around noon. Julieta put on her bathing suit to go to the beach. When Manolo saw her coming out of the bathroom in the tiny bright pink bikini, he grabbed her, took off her bikini and made love to her again. Then they took a shower together, went to swim in the pool and spent the rest of the afternoon resting on recliners next to the pool. About seven, after watching the sundown, one of the most beautiful things to watch when you are next to the sea, they went back to change into evening, albeit casual clothes, for a dinner in LaBrasserie and wild dancing in a different disco. Then back to the hotel for another session of love-making.

By now Manolo was again cocky and sure of himself. He had already made up his mind, he would have as much fun as he could get out of this trip, then, he would dump her. Julieta noticed a change, but assumed that it was just that now he felt more at ease with her, more intimate.

Sunday, after waking up late and having a swim and late lunch, they went back to the suite to prepare their bags. But before packing, they made love once more, this time calmly and tenderly. Julieta felt reassured.

Afterwards, they drove back to the airport, dropped the rental car and flew back to Mexico City on the Bonanza. They said good-bye in the airport. Julieta noticed certain coldness in

Manolo that she could not fully understand, but decided not to say anything until they saw each other again.

By the time Julieta got home, her mother was already there and made a comment about her sunburn. Julieta blushed a little and just answered that she had fallen asleep in the sun in Cuernavaca. Mrs. Velasco looked at Julieta and a mother's instinct told her that something was not totally right.

10

BREAKING UP

The whole week went by and Manolo did not call Julieta. He knew that she would be expecting his call because, although they had not said anything but a short good-bye on Sunday night, they had been going out almost every day for lunch before the trip. It was logical that Julieta would expect him to call. Without recognizing it to himself, Manolo was hoping Julieta would call. Not Monday or Tuesday, he knew she had a lot of dignity and also that she was a little shy, as he had discovered. But, by Wednesday, Manolo found himself checking his various voice mails every ten or fifteen minutes and checking and re-checking his cell phone to ascertain it was working properly. Also, he found himself wanting to go to his office early to see if Julieta had called him there.

The next Wednesday, he started asking Monica Gutierrez, his secretary, if he had had any calls with a little more insistence. Monica, who read him as an open book, noticed the trend. On Friday, when Manolo walked in, asked if there had been anything important and Monica answered in the negative, he went into his office and from there he shouted, "Have I had any calls?"

Monica responded: "Manolo, you know that I always leave

your messages on top of your desk." She was on a first name basis with Manolo, something quite unusual in the very formal atmosphere of the Mexican business circles, partially because she was really more the manager of the office than a secretary, and partially because she had an affair with Manolo long before being his secretary.

"That's right, but I just wondered--" he said, walking out into his waiting room, where Monica had her desk.

"Wondered if Julieta had called?"

"Well... not really," he said, then after a pause, "She hasn't called, right?"

"No Manolo, Julieta has not called and probably will not call until you call her. Have you called her?"

"No. I don't really want to go out with her anymore, just wondered if she was going to be difficult to get rid of."

"I don't think you are going to have any trouble getting rid of a girl like Julieta," said Monica, who had met her a few times.

Manolo did not respond, but it was obvious that he was upset by Monica's comment. The rest of the morning he spent in a sullen silence broken only when Monica passed him phone calls from his friends, who were already organizing three-martini lunches for that day and for partying all weekend. At some point, the phone rang and it was one of Monica's friends with some gossip. While Monica was speaking she could see that Manolo had gotten up from behind his desk, peeked into the waiting room, saw her on the phone, and returned to his desk. After Monica hung up, Manolo hollered all the way from his desk: "That call was not for me, was it Monica?"

"No, Manolo, it was one of my girlfriends," answered Monica, by now a little exasperated.

If Manolo was expecting Julieta to call, he was in for a big disappointment. Three weeks went by and Julieta never called. Manolo assumed that if he were to call her, she would jump sky-high and accept to date with him again, but he didn't know it for sure and his macho pride felt hurt. He had dumped plenty of girls in the past and was used to their calling and calling long after he had stopped calling them. Not once before had he had such an experience with a girl.

Then, on the fourth week, something happened. It was a Friday, the busiest day of the week for Monica who was in charge, among other things, of preparing and distributing the payroll. On Fridays, Manolo would get to the office no later than eleven-thirty. The banks in Mexico City closed early and the workers had to be paid in cash, so Monica would normally prepare the check for Manolo's signature by two o'clock at the latest, in order to have one of the messengers go cash it to the bank and bring back the money.

That particular Friday was extremely busy. The company had been working on a couple of new landscaping projects and there were a lot of day-laborers that had to be paid, in addition to the regular crews who handled only the maintenance work. Monica had gotten to the office before eight that morning. When the mail came in, around ten-thirty, she didn't even pay attention to the bunch of envelopes, only sorted out those that were addressed to her or to different departments of the company, like accounting, purchasing, etc. The small firm had only Monica, two junior secretaries and a receptionist, plus four errand-boys, who acted also as messengers and collectors. The company used outside consultants for almost all its bookkeeping and records, which helped maintain the overhead very low and make it extremely profitable. After picking out those that she needed to handle, Monica left all the other envelopes on top of Manolo's desk.

Shortly after one fifteen, Monica could hear the whining roar of Manolo's Porsche in the yard and, sure enough, a minute later Manolo appeared in her office. He asked her the usual questions about anything important and, seeing that she was swamped with work, he walked into his office after saying: "Bring me the check when it's ready."

About twenty minutes later, Monica finished her calculations, wrote and cut the check and walked into Manolo's office. As soon as she walked through the open door, she knew something was wrong. Manolo was sitting at his elegant Lopez-Morton desk with a sheet of pale pink stationery in his hand and an empty stare. When Monica walked in, Manolo turned his ashen-white face to her and put the letter face down over his desk.

"Something wrong Manolo?" asked Monica.

"No, why do you ask?" he lied openly, but almost immediately continued: "Well... actually... yes. The bitch is threatening to commit suicide," he said, the words hissing out of his mouth.

Monica could see that he was really scared, but also extraordinarily angry. She did not know what to say. What can you say in a case like this? She tried comforting Manolo, "I do not really think she is going to do it, she is probably only trying to get your attention." Amazingly, neither one had mentioned the name of Julieta, but Monica instinctively knew they were talking about her.

"I think she might really try it. Didn't I tell you I had noticed something strange about this girl," he said, knowing full well that he had never spoken anything to Monica about Julieta being strange.

Monica was a pragmatist, she could not help it; that was just the way she was. She had acted pragmatically after having her affair with Manolo. When he dumped her, she had been really heartbroken. Manolo was not only wealthy and a member of one of the most prominent families of Mexico, but he was also very good-looking and knew how to treat a girl and make her feel like a queen. Monica overcame her bitterness after being subjected to 'the treatment' by Manolo. About one year later, she ran into him in the Pink Zone and he offered her a job as his secretary. The pragmatist in Monica accepted and now she had become more the manager of the company than a secretary.

This time, her practical sense prevailed and Monica simply said, in a matter-of-fact voice, "Look Manolo, let's assume that she really does commit suicide, what the heck, you were going to get rid of her anyway, just forget all about it."

"I guess you're right. But, you are a cold-hearted bitch, you know that?"

"Sure, that's the only way to survive a son-of-a-bitch macho like you," said Monica, adding a smile to soften the cussing.

Manolo smiled back, but Monica could see that his smile was forced. 'He is really scared,' –she thought–.

At around nine, with the lights in downtown Houston shining through the marvelous view of the wall-sized window, Roberto and Manolo moved from Roberto's desk to the seating area located on the other side of Roberto's huge private office. They were both very tired. They had been talking for over twelve hours. Roberto sat on one of the individual wing sofas with Manolo to his left, seated on the English button couch, as he invited Manolo to continue his narrative.

Next Monday, Manolo came in to his office at his usual time, around twelve. He looked pale and haggard and Monica deduced that maybe this time all his macho-posturing was giving way to a sentiment of love. Could it be that he was in love with this Julieta girl after all? For a while, it had certainly seemed that he was really in love with her.

Manolo asked the usual questions and then walked into his office and closed the door behind him. 'Definitively, he's not acting normal today,' –thought Monica–. He seldom closed the door to his office.

The morning went by pretty normal, by two-thirty Monica announced through the intercom that she was going to lunch. Manolo had not given any indications that he planned to go out, which was also contrary to his custom, so Monica ventured an invitation. "Do you care to go out for lunch, Manolo? I'll buy."

"Thanks, Monica," he answered, "But I'll pass this time, I am not feeling well, seems like I'm coming down with the flu, or something."

That afternoon, when Monica returned at four-thirty, the Porsche was still parked outside under the two-car carport of the yard when Monica parked her Toyota Camry next to it. It seemed like Manolo had not been out. When she walked into the office, Manolo's door was still closed. She announced she was back through the intercom and Manolo just answered: "Fine."

It was around 6:45 p.m. when the phone, which had been unusually silent that Monday, rang in Monica's office. She jumped a little, the office had been in an eerie silence with Manolo, who would normally be hollering instructions to Monica through his open door, closed behind the door in his office.

"Yes Clara, who is it?" asked Monica of the receptionist who, in the next room, was in charge of answering the phone board exchange.

"It's a Mrs. Velasco, Monica, she is asking for Mr. Pardo," answered the girl.

Monica felt a strange sensation in her stomach. 'Mrs. Velasco? Maybe it's Julieta, she thought, but aloud she simply said to the girl, "I'll take it Clara." She punched a button and answered: "Yes ma'am, can I help you?"

A voice she had never heard before answered: "No, you cannot, I want to speak with Mr. Manuel Pardo." The voice was soft, but Monica could feel a tone of pain with a touch of confrontation. She thought Manolo would not want to take the call, but she had to ask him. "Will you hold a minute please ma'am, I think he is in conference." Monica punched the intercom and Manolo answered, "Yes?"

"Manolo, it's Julieta's mother, do you want to take the call or do you want me to handle it." She fully expected Manolo to ask her to handle it, but to her surprise she heard Manolo say, "I'll take it." She transferred the call and waited.

Monica was a pragmatist, but she was also a woman and curiosity won. She waited a couple of minutes and then, taking a folder with some papers that she had to show to Manolo at some point, she opened the door to Manolo's office and walked in. Manolo was still on the phone and did not even turn his head to look at Monica. He was saying: "...She never even gave a hint of that, Mrs. Velasco. We had an argument the weekend she went to Cuernavaca and I did not talk to her ever again." Monica, who knew about the weekend in Acapulco, could not help but admire the coolness with which Manolo was lying. After listening for a moment, Manolo responded, "Mrs. Velasco, I am terribly sorry, you have my deepest sympathy, but I do not believe my friend-ship with Julieta had anything to do with this. Now, if I could help financially in any way, I would be--" he stopped in the middle of the sentence, looked at the phone and then softly placed it down, it was obvious that Mrs. Velasco had hung-up on him. He turned to Monica with a face that was still haggard but seemed more collected than when she saw him in the morning and said to her: "You are not going to believe this, that stupid girl got pregnant and wanted to hang it around my neck, then she panicked at her mother's reaction and killed herself. I never thought she would actually do it when she threatened it, but she actually did." He said it with a tone of disbelief.

Monica felt as if she was about to be sick. She had met Julieta only a few times while she was dating Manolo and Manolo would come to drop his car to then drive in Julieta's car. Julieta seemed like a really nice girl, extremely pretty and intelligent. Monica even thought that maybe this time Manolo was going to get hitched.

Now, hearing that she had killed herself and that she was pregnant, Monica felt her eyes watering. "How could you tell her mother that she never gave any indication of suicide, when just last Friday you received that letter?" she said, guessing, rather than knowing what the conversation had been about.

"What?" answered Manolo, who reacted like if something had stung him, "You yourself told me to ignore her and not give a hoot about her threats. Are you now blaming it on me as well?"

"I'm not blaming anything on anybody, but how can you be so cold-hearted?"

"Now you call me cold-hearted. I seem to remember you were the one who was cold-hearted last Friday. Anyway, what did you want me to do, tell the mother about the letter and then have her blame me for not trying to stop Julieta from committing suicide. She is already blaming me for the baby. Anyway, I burned the letter, I do not want anything to do with this."

"Did Julieta tell you in the letter that she was pregnant?" asked Monica.

"She just said that her period was late and that she was scared that she might be expecting a baby, she said that she could not face it and was going to kill herself rather than wait to be sure if she was really pregnant."

"What exactly did she say?" said Monica, now lamenting not having asked to be allowed to read the letter.

"I don't even remember exactly. Just what I told you." Responded Manolo, contradicting himself.

11

ATTACK

R aul was hanging at the usual corner with the usual crowd when his cell phone went off. He carried the phone hanging from his waist like an old west gunslinger. It helped conceal the Smith & Wesson .38 snub nose revolver that he carried slightly ahead of the phone under his shirt, Raul was left-handed. Of course Raul did not have a concealed weapons license, no way he would have gotten one with his rap sheet.

Raul opened the cell phone and answered, "Hi," his usual greeting.

"Raul?"

"Yeah."

"The boss needs you to take care of a guy."

"How bad."

"Well, you know, just give him a scare, nothing really serious."

"Sure. Who's the guy?"

"You're going to love this one. He's an attorney. I'll send you the name and address in a couple of days." His interlocutor knew how much Raul hated attorneys ever since, in Raul's opinion, a personal injury attorney who represented his mother after a car wreck had cheated her.

"Great. Consider it done," said Raul and closed the phone.

———

The next couple of days were busy for Raul while he carefully picked his mates for the contract. He had been born in Durango, Mexico, and brought to Houston illegally by his parents as a baby, together with his older siblings. His father had gotten work as a waiter in a Mexican restaurant, while his mother worked odd jobs, mainly as domestic help for well-off Anglos. In 1985 the whole family had gotten their papers under the Amnesty program. In 1997 they all had become naturalized U.S. citizens, which was lucky for Raul because by then his criminal record was non-existent, although he had already ventured deeply into gang related activities.

It was good that Raul was a U.S. citizen, because the Republican controlled Congress had started passing laws as a conservative backlash to the Amnesty. The laws enacted provided that any alien caught in offenses even as minor as shoplifting would be deportable upon conviction. Those laws also established administrative deportations under which the convicted alien could be deported after an interview with an INS officer without the intervention of an immigration judge.

But Raul was already a U.S. citizen by the time his official rap sheet began and, although he had received more than one severe scolding from several judges, his known crimes had not yet reached the level of requiring incarceration.

On the second day, one of the members of the gang walked to him at their usual corner and gave him a folded piece of paper without saying a word. Raul knew that it had to be the name of and instructions to get to the attorney he was supposed to rough-up. Sure enough, once he got back home, he opened the folded paper and read: "Roberto Duran, Tranquility Park garage, the side under the Bank of America Building, tonight. He will be working late. Get him while he walks to a silver gray BMW Z4M parked in space 745 on the second basement, near the entrance to the Alley Theatre."

"Shit!" muttered Raul. He hated Anglos and he didn't mind hitting on Africans, but a Hispanic... 'Well, what the hell. If the guy made the boss mad, he deserves it,' –he thought–.

Raul planned to be accompanied by two of his most trusted and toughest friends. The boss paid very good money for the various services of the gang, ranging from drug deliveries to beatings of competitors, and he had to be kept pleased. Who was this final "boss" nobody in Houston really knew. They just knew that he was in Mexico and sent an endless amount of cash to help make the gang the most affluent one in Pasadena. Raul drove a 2006 Chevrolet Impala painted in a very bright cherry color, all souped-up and equipped with the latest air shocks to make it spring up or down at will. The car was almost standard issue for a gang member, only that newer and more luxuriously appointed than the usual.

That evening, the three members of the gang got into the parking garage by having a fourth member drive in and then leave while the three others remained inside and hid the best they could. Raul had already located the parking space and ascertained that the sports BMW was there. Now it was just a matter of waiting.

Manolo finished his narrative around eleven thirty that night. Roberto remained silent for a minute, then asked, "Did you ever think that you were a lucky bastard having found one of those exceptional women who care enough about you to tell you the truth?"

"Come on, Roberto, are you going to blame Julieta's death on me also?" replied Manolo, obviously upset by the comment.

"No, but you are, aren't you?"

"Well... yes... I guess to some extent I feel that maybe if I had tried to stop her, she would still be alive."

"That is a moot proposition now Manolo," said Roberto, "The issue is, why are you blaming yourself? I sense that you feel more than a normal amount of guilt."

Manolo's face became pale and he whispered: "No, I don't... not really."

"Anyway," said Roberto, "It sure gives a good motive for anyone who loved the girl to harm you. The reason I asked you about her was because Luis Gil, your grandfather's chief investigator --"

"Yeah, I know who he is."

"--Okay, well he suggested that maybe Julieta's father, being a drug trafficker, set up a trap to punish you for her death."

Manolo's face became paler.

"I imagine that you told Luis what Julieta said about her father," continued Roberto.

"No, I never said anything to anybody. How was it that Luis Gil found out about Julieta's father being a trafficker?" responded Manolo.

"I couldn't tell you. I only know that Luis found out, and he feels that is what might have happened. You already assured me before the detention hearing that you had no idea whatsoever that the cocaine was in your bags. It follows that someone put it there and that 'someone' has to be a person who would like for you to be hurt."

"I guess you're right, Roberto," responded Manolo, his face still pale.

"Well, it's pretty late, let's go. Do you have a car or do you want me to drive you home?"

"No, my grandfather's car is waiting for me downstairs," responded Manolo.

They went down all the way to the first floor's lobby, which was totally empty at that time. Roberto decided to walk Manolo over to the car. They came out of the building into Smith street. A silver gray Lexus 450, almost identical, except for the color, to the one that had driven Roberto around in Mexico City, was waiting at the curb. Two men seemed to be asleep inside with the windows partially down. Manolo approached the driver's window and knocked on it. The men straightened up immediately and the click of the electric locks could be heard as they both got out of the car, the man from the passenger side came around while the driver opened the left rear door for Manolo to climb in.

They said good-bye and Roberto used his card-key to go back into the building. He took the escalators to go down two levels and walked in the deserted tunnel to the Tranquility Park Garage. Once there he went to where his reserved parking space was. The garage was brightly lit but totally deserted at that time. Roberto knew that the security of the garage was pretty tight so he was not concerned by the emptiness. He sometimes worked very late on some cases and the garage was a pretty safe place.

He turned a corner to where his gray convertible BMW was parked in his reserved space, it was the only car left on that side of the garage. He walked towards it and, suddenly, he felt a drop of water fall on the rear part of his head. He looked up and back to the ceiling because Houston had been in a dry spell with no rain. Sure enough the ceiling was dry. He was a little surprised, but thought nothing of it until when he was turning around to continue to walk to his car. He then saw with the corner of the eye someone move next to one of the walls. He turned again and now he could see three young men coming fast toward him.

They had been walking parallel to him but behind the wall. One of them had something in his hand and the other two had both hands inside the pockets of their leather jackets. Roberto had been in enough tight spots in his life to recognize that danger was imminent and very serious. Had it not been for that drop of water falling on his head, the men, who wore expensive-looking sneakers, would have been able to attack him by surprise from the back. The attackers seemed to be as surprised by Roberto looking at them as Roberto was by seeing them. They had obviously expected to be able to make a surprise attack.

Now, they hesitated for a split second, while Roberto did not. All his training in martial arts and in the Special Forces in Vietnam stressed the fact that, if you are sure you will be attacked, you are better off attacking first. At 56, Roberto was not as elastic as in his youth, but his reflexes were still marvelous. Moving surprisingly fast for a man his build, he took two steps toward the attacker on the right. He was the one whose hand held something, a bicycle chain it happened to be, so he was the most dangerous because he was ready to fight. Roberto turned slightly sideways and at the same time sent a low sidekick to the knee of the left knee of the man. He could hear the vicious noise of breaking leg bones. When the young man bent over with the pain, Roberto sent a karate chop with the knuckle of his right fist, cutting the air downwards from his left shoulder down to the left temple of the man. One of the other two had pulled out a short baton from his jacket. In a split second, Roberto saw the one still unarmed hesitating while the other one attacked Roberto. Roberto swirled to one side to bypass the attacking man and went for the one who appeared to hesitate. He was the most dangerous, because he might be trying to get a more deadly weapon.

Which was true in Raul's case. After learning that Roberto was Hispanic, Raul had decided to be a little soft on the guy. 'A baton will be enough to kick his butt,' –he had thought–. Now, seeing the dangerousness of his intended victim, Raul tried to pull out his Smith & Wesson.

He would never get a chance. After bypassing the attacking

man, Roberto sent a straight kick with his right leg to the neck of Raul. The kick hit on the center of Adam's apple and Raul fell down like a bunch of rags. When Roberto turned around to face the third assailant, he heard the shout of "Freeze!"

With the corner of his eye, he saw a security guard with the face of a high-school freshman and with his gun drawn and in position to shoot. He swiftly threw himself to the ground. He was more afraid of an untrained security guard with a gun than of the other man with a baton. Sure enough, the instant he hit the ground, he heard the explosion of a shot. It was probably a .38, but it sounded like a Howitzer cannon in the empty echo-filled space of the parking garage. The guard was not only a rookie but a bad-shot too. The third assailant, unharmed by the shot, started running toward the wall on one side. The guard took five shots more at him, missing all of them, while the man disappeared behind the wall. Before the man disappeared, Roberto could hear the empty click of the hammer hitting two times against the mechanism of the gun. The guard approached Roberto, who was still crouching on the ground and asked: "Are you all right sir?"

"Yes," responded Roberto, "It would be a good idea if you keep an eye on these two, if they get up." The two attackers were sprawled on the floor. A stream of blood was coming out of the mouth and nose of Raul and the other seemed to be in Valhalla. "I'll try to see if I can catch the other one."

The guard obeyed. Roberto ran to the wall and looked behind, but the man had disappeared into thin air. Roberto walked back to the scene, where the security guard nervously held his .38 toward the bodies on the ground without realizing that the gun, a six-shooter, was now empty and useless. There was no problem, the two men were barely alive, as the paramedics stated after an ambulance came, called by a second security guard who arrived at the scene shortly after the first one.

After the ambulance was called, Roberto walked over to the BMW, placed his briefcase inside the trunk and pulling out his cell phone called Lulu, his wife. He had called her from the office around eight-thirty after he saw that the conversation with Manolo was going to take an awful lot more time than he had expected. Lulu was a night person and oftentimes she would be up until one or two in the morning, praying or watching T.V.

The phone rang only once, Lulu answered: "Hello," with her sweet voice like that of a child. That was one of the things that kept Roberto in love with her.

"Muñequita--" started Roberto in Spanish, but he was interrupted by an avalanche from Lulu.

"Now, don't you tell me you are still not coming home Roberto, you cannot continue doing this. You have to understand that you have to rest," she said, her tone not childish now, but highly aggressive.

Roberto suppressed a smile at the thought of how easily the little sweet bird could become a lioness, while explaining to her what had just happened. Lulu reacted just as Roberto expected and they both made a short prayer in praise of the Lord for His protection.

The ambulance came. The police came too. Roberto stated to them that there had been an attempt to mug him. One of the police officers knew Roberto from the courts and simply gave Roberto his card and asked him to try to arrange

for a statement to be taken of him the following day. "These two guys are in pretty bad shape, counselor," he said, "If they expire, it would be better to have statements of all those involved."

"Sure officer, I'll see to it tomorrow, first thing."

"Thanks counselor, these guys never knew what hit them, if they had known that you used to be in the Special Forces, they probably would have taken their business some place else."

Roberto smiled and then walked back to the place where he felt the drop of water fall on his hair. As he had seen before the ceiling was dry, now he could see the floor was also completely dry. He bowed his head, put his hands together in front of his chest and made a short prayer of thanks to the Lord for his protection.

The police detective, who was looking in his direction, had a puzzled look on his face when Roberto looked up after his prayer. Roberto just smiled to him and the detective smiled back just shaking his head a little.

12

THE TRIGGERMAN

That same night, at about nine, Luis Gil was seated at his desk in his office on the fourth floor of the main building of Bancomer Center. During the past two days he had gotten in touch with his contacts in the underworld and was waiting for news from them. After talking to Roberto Duran on the phone the day before to give him the information on the Caprice, Luis continued trying to find out as much as possible about Julieta and her father.

He also had many more security concerns to attend for Bancomer, so that night he was working on them, dictating memorandums for Teresa his secretary to type and send to the different departments of the giant organization. Like most high-placed Mexicans, he worked really late. Almost every day his light would still be on at 9 p.m. It was shortly before nine, so it was within his normal working time. Teresa had planned to leave at around nine-thirty, after finishing the memos. Suddenly, the phone rang and Teresa hollered through the open door from the reception, "Commander Gil, it is 'Sabandija' on line one."

Teresa weighed nearly three hundred pounds, and was in her late sixties. She had been his first secretary once he became a

Commander in the Judicial Police, and after her, Luis did not want anybody else. When he quit the force, Teresa left also, to work as his private secretary. She was a mountain of a woman, energetic, trustworthy and full of authority, a feature that made Luis jokingly say that in a previous life she had been a master sergeant in the French Foreign Legion. But she could also be the sweetest and most adorable of persons. Sometimes Luis suspected that he was slightly in love with the woman, a platonic love of course. Maybe she symbolized the mother he had never really come to know.

Luis picked up the phone. He recognized the voice of Sabandija, 'the Lizard.' In Spanish the word has a connotation also of a bug, of a crawling beast, of someone despicable and feared. Sabandija, whose real name nobody knew, had been one of his informers in the police. True to his nickname, he was despicable and would sell his mother for money. But he was also extremely valuable as an informer. He had ears everywhere and connections with everybody. He was very careful with his dealings and also very lucky. Both features had allowed him to survive in a world where most informers get killed soon.

"Commander," he said in his hoarse voice, product of too much alcohol, chain-smoking and too little sleep, "About that information you needed, I have something for you."

"Good Sabandija, come right over," responded Luis, teasing him, because he knew how paranoid Sabandija was.

"No way Commander, you want the info, you come over here."

"Fine Sabandija, where do you want to meet," said Luis while he saw the burly figure of Teresa standing on the doorway to his office.

"You know where Plaza Garibaldi is?"

Of course, Luis and almost everybody else in Mexico City knew that Garibaldi was the square where most of the mariachi groups gathered at night to wait for patrons who would come and hire them to go serenade their fair maids. But it was also in the heart of Tepito, the rough and tumble 'barrio' of the City that was considered extremely dangerous, particularly if you happen to be a police officer.

When Luis responded, "Of course I know where Garibaldi is," Teresa grimaced and shook her head. Luis ignored her while Sabandija gave him directions to meet him in a dark alley a few blocks away from Garibaldi Square.

When he hung up, Teresa said in her authoritarian tone, "You are not going at this time of the night to Garibaldi, Commander, too many people there remember you as a Fed," Luis had asked her several times to call him by his first name and Teresa had attempted it a few times, but always reverted to the respectful 'Commander.'

"Come on Teresa, we need that information, this is a real big case for Don Jose, you know."

"It doesn't matter, you are not going."

"Okay, let's bargain," said Luis in a conciliatory tone, which he knew was the best to convince Teresa, "I'll go, but not in my car, I'm driving the Thunderbird and it's too flashy, I'll take your Focus."

"Now I will not only lose my boss, but also my car will probably get smashed by whoever kills you," responded Teresa in a sad voice while shaking her head and walking toward her purse to take her keys and hand them over to Luis.

"Thanks Terry, you are a real treasure," said Luis pulling out two 9 mm magazines from a drawer in his desk. He got up, took the keys from her and kissed her on the cheek, "I'll be back before you finish typing those memos," he lied.

"What kind of artillery are you carrying?" she asked before he walked out through the door.

"The usual, the Beretta and this baby," replied Luis patting his right trouser leg, where he always carried a .38 special Smith & Wesson air weight snub-nose revolver.

"There is a Rugers .357 magnum and plenty of ammo in the glove compartment, if you need it," said Teresa, "And be sure to come back in one piece... and be sure to bring my car back without a scratch," she hollered, while Luis was about to get in the elevator.

Luis felt glad to be driving an unobtrusive four door Ford Focus when he went into Tepito. The thought of driving his '57 Thunderbird convertible on these streets was not too reassuring. He drove by Garibaldi Square, turning where Sabandija had instructed him to turn. He continued five blocks and located the bar that Sabandija gave him as a reference, then, he had to backtrack two blocks before finding a parking place.

Most of the buildings of the 'barrio' were two and three-story Spanish colonial constructions that had been palaces in their heyday but now were the rundown and patchy equivalent of the housing projects of American cities. Parking was a problem because the old palaces had been turned each into myriads of apartments and none had parking garages. People simply had to look for a place to park their cars on the streets. Amazingly, the cars you could see parked on those streets seemed out of place, you would have expected to see them in a high-income area, but not in Tepito.

Frozen rents and a system of property that did not give any relief to landowners but neither solved the problems of tenants had turned this area of the City into a slum inhabited by the toughest breed of people. Luis knew many of them well. They were proud and brave. Excellent friends, but very lousy enemies. Some of the most notable prize-fighters that had given renown to Mexican boxing had been born and raised here in Tepito, and also many of the worst criminals and lowlifes.

'Probably that explains why you see these cars,' –thought

Luis– while he negotiated a tight turn to be able to win a space that was being left by another car leaving. He parked the car and, before opening the door, he pulled out the Beretta from his Burns-Martin shoulder holster and checked the magazine. Before inserting the magazine, he got an extra round and put it in the chamber, cocking the gun and returning the hammer to its safe position. Then he inserted the magazine and put the safe. He checked the two extra magazines that he had put in his jacket pockets before leaving the office. All of his ammo were dum-dum. Although he did not expect anybody to, if someone tried to mess with him, that someone would get badly hurt.

He got out of the car, walked the two blocks to the alley where Sabandija was supposed to be waiting for him and peeked into the dark alley. Sure enough, he saw the silhouette of a man standing next to one of the walls, a few steps away.

"Sabandija," he whispered.

"Yes, Commander, come over."

Luis walked cautiously to the man in the dark and asked, "So, what's so important that you want to tell me?"

"It's not so much what I want to tell you, but who I want you to meet," said Sabandija, motioning to another man next to him who had been hidden by the shadows.

Luis's heart missed a beat, he had not seen the other man and shuddered to think of how easily he could have been ambushed in spite of all his preparations. He said, "You never said there would be someone else Sabandija, that is not healthy. What if I had started shooting like crazy?"

"No, Commander, you are too civilized for that," said Sabandija, dismissing the upset tone in the voice of Luis. "My friend here has a little story that he wants you to hear."

The other man stepped out of the shadows. Luis could see that he was as tall as himself, over six feet tall, lean but muscular, with the very dark skin of the 'costeños,' the people from the coast. His curly hair revealed a good deal of African blood, not uncommon on the coastal areas of Mexico.

The man said: "Good night, Commander, my name of course is not important, but Sabandija here, I owe him a couple of favors. He tells me you are a good friend of him and need some help. I believe I may provide you with the information you are looking for."

"Yes?" answered Luis questioningly.

"Why don't we go to the bar across the street," suggested Sabandija, his thirst always unquenchable.

"No, better stay here," said Luis, who was already pretty unnerved.

"As you want." Sabandija obviously would have preferred to get some drinks.

The other man said, "Yes, it's better to stay here. Well sir, this is the story. I am... well, you could call me 'an enforcer.'" Luis thought that sure enough the man had all the appearances of a triggerman. "Anyway," continued the man, "The other night, I was sent to turn the screws on some tough guys who had displeased my boss. I did not know who the people were, so they sent this guy with me, to identify them. We had to sit inside my car for several hours, waiting for those guys to show up, so this man gets bored and starts asking for a drink. I always carry a cooler full of beer in the trunk of my car for stalk-outs, so I gave him some beer and his tongue loosened. He started griping about how the boss wasted some perfectly good cocaine in setting up a trap for a rich boy who had offended him. The man was really upset. He's a junkie, and the idea of throwing away cocaine made him sick. When Sabandija here told me about the grandson of Don Jose Gomez-Iglesias, well, I added two plus two and--"

The interest of Luis had heightened greatly, he interrupted, "Who is your boss?"

"That, my friend, I cannot tell you, because I do not know."

"What do you mean you don't know."

"Just that, sir. Whoever he may be, he doesn't know who I am, and I don't want to know who he is. In my profession it's better that way."

Luis understood, he just nodded and asked, "What about this man who was with you, does he know who the boss is?"

"I don't think so, but you would have to ask him. Now, I've heard rumors, I can tell you about those."

"Sure, but first please continue with your story, sorry I interrupted you."

"Well, my man there in the car starts telling me, you know, about how the boss had gotten some counterfeit Louis Vuitton bags here in Tepito and sent them to him in Houston. How they used the bags to set-up a trap by bribing some guys up there in the airport of Houston to change the clothes from the set of bags that the rich jerk was carrying and put them in the counterfeit bags. He almost cried when he told me of how he personally supervised how they had hidden the cocaine in the counterfeit set, before taking the bags to the airport. Afterwards, they had a snitch, who is really working for his boss, call U.S. Customs and tell them that the young guy was trying to smuggle several 'keys' of coke."

"Good deal for the snitch," commented Luis, "He gains points with U.S. Customs and at the same time he pleases the boss."

"That's exactly right," said the man. "So, that's the story, I believe that is what you wanted to know."

"Yes, I already suspected it had to be that way. It's great to have a confirmation. But now I need a lot more information to give to the attorney who is representing the young man in the United States," said Luis.

"Like what?"

"Like who is this mysterious boss."

"Well, I told you, the only thing I have is rumors."

"That's good enough, for the time being."

"Well, what I have heard is that he is very high up in the business community."

"In the business community?" asked Luis with surprise. Like many people in Mexico, he sometimes conjectured that some high government officials had to be involved in drug-trafficking, but he had never heard rumors of an important businessman being involved.

"That is what I've heard," said the man. "That he was trained in Cuba as a terrorist many years ago as part of the group of young students who in 1968 were part of the student riots in the University of Mexico, you remember?"

"Of course," said Luis. Nobody who lived in Mexico City at that time would ever forget that year. It was shortly before the Olympic Games of 1968 that were held in Mexico City. Students organized a strike using some pretext or other, Luis did not remember what. The movement snow-balled until the Army moved-in to retake the University. After that there was another attempt to create chaos, but the government beheaded it with a blood bath in Tlatelolco Square.

"They say that he learned in Cuba the techniques to organize in cells," continued the man while Luis remembered those days, "Small, tightly-knit groups where you only know a handful of others. They say that he uses the system now to conduct his drug business. It must be working, because I have not ever heard about anybody who knows who he is. They all say that it might be this guy, or that other guy, but for sure, nobody knows."

"What about the man who was with you that night?" asked Luis, "You said he may know who the boss is?"

"Again, you would have to ask him about that. But, it may help you to know that he mentioned he gets his orders from the 'Pentagon,' whatever that means," answered the man.

Luis pondered for a short while on what the triggerman had said. It was obvious that the Pentagon was not the Department of Defense Building in Washington, but he had no idea of what it could be. He did not think he could get any more information from the man. Just to satisfy his curiosity he asked, "Not to be nosy, but what happened with those tough guys that you were stalking that night?"

"Well... it's kind of funny," said the trigger man, "My contact told me that the boss had found out that in one of the cells of the organization, made-up of only four guys, there was one who was cheating. The boss did not know which of the four it was, so he ordered the four men killed."

"And...?" said Luis with surprise in his voice.

"The four guys showed up after several hours of stalking them, not together of course. First we got one, then another, then another, and finally we got the fourth one," responded the man in a matter of fact voice.

"You mean that you killed the four men just because one of them was supposedly cheating on the boss?" asked Luis incredulously.

"Sure, that's what I do for a living."

13

THE ROAD TO CUERNAVACA

L uis walked back into his office weary and exhausted. It was already past eleven. Teresa was asleep on the couch of her office so Luis shook her gently to wake her up.

"What happened?" she asked with a sleepy voice.

Luis told her briefly about the strange meeting with the trigger man and then sent her home, not without telling her: "Don't come in tomorrow Terry, I'll manage without you."

"Don't count on it," she replied picking up all her things and getting ready to leave, "I'll be here, just do not expect me before eleven-thirty in the morning."

"Fine," replied Luis with his typical grin. He knew Teresa would not miss a day's work. As far as he remembered, she had never missed a day, she worked even with bad colds.

After Teresa left, Luis looked at his watch, he was dying to tell Roberto about what he had just learned, but thought that it was already too late to call him at home. Just then, the telephone in his office rang. It was Roberto.

"Hi, friend, I didn't think you would still answer," said Roberto, who was calling the office number of Luis, "I was only going to leave you a message."

"I was thinking of calling you to tell you what just happened, but I also thought it was too late to call. But, go ahead, tell me, what happened?"

"I was talking with Manolo all day long."

"Great, did you find out something?"

"Lots, but I will write a memo first thing tomorrow morning and federal express it to you. What about your story?"

Luis told him about the triggerman and his strange story and Roberto just said, "It sure is consistent with what happened to me."

"Your turn, tell me what happened," said Luis.

"There has just been an attempt to mug me in the parking garage of my building."

"What, just now?" said Luis with unbelief.

"Right this very moment. I am still inside the garage. I am convinced this is connected with Manolo's case."

"Very probably. What are you going to do?"

"Right now, go home and sleep, I am exhausted, but I wanted to tell you because I have a feeling that we will be forced to find out who that son of a bitch is and stop him dead on his tracks," said Roberto, and Luis could tell that he was really upset.

"Sure thing. I'll get on to it tomorrow and will call you. Bye now."

"Bye, Luis."

The next morning, back at his desk at nine, Luis started a new round of calls to his informants and wrote a short memo to Don Jose telling him of the conversation with Roberto and with the triggerman. After that, he went over some of the paperwork that always seems to pile up on your desk. Shortly before 11, bored to death by the paper work and unable to joke with Teresa, who had not arrived yet, Luis saw that the weather outside was glorious and aware that his contacts would reach him via his cell phone, he decided to go down to the parking garage on the third level of the basement of Bancomer Center and get into his T-bird.

He had planned to meet with Sabandija for lunch at Arroyo's restaurant to pay him off. The wheels of information are expensive and demanding. Prompt payment is necessary to keep them running.

The day was one of those gloriously beautiful days of Mexico City. The sun was shining and the smog was very low. The 'City of Eternal Spring' as Mexico City is sometimes called, was honoring her name that day. The temperature was 72 degrees and the fresh air felt wonderful. The ragtop was down and Luis could hear the purr of the big 8-cylinder engine through the four tailpipes of his T-bird.

Although it was in collector's shape, for the experts it was not the real classic. For connoisseurs, only the '55 and '56 models are the 'classic' classic. The '57 is considered a little spurious because the tail fins are slightly twisted outward. Also, this bird in particular was not a classic in a different sense. Luis had souped it up considerably. The original 289 cubic-inch engine had been substituted for a 5.7 liter Ford Interceptor engine capable of developing 425 horsepower, the largest stock engine Ford manufactured. Luis added twin Weber carburetors and oversized headers. The transmission and differential were also changed to install a 5-speed manual transmission coupled to a limited-slip differential, instead of the original automatic transmission of the car. The suspension had been improved with independent McPherson struts and other modifications, which had turned the very docile T-bird into a lion. In short, the graceful but indolent Thunderbird had been turned into a real sports car.

Luis drove on Insurgentes Avenue to the south.

Perhaps, if the weather had not been that good, the idea of having 'carnitas' and 'guacamole' with freshly prepared 'tortillas' at Arroyo's so appealing, and the purr of the big Interceptor engine so nice to hear, Luis would have noticed that he was being followed. But he did not. He was totally abstracted in enjoying the ride. He drove-by Arroyo's and continued to the south.

He had decided to go to 'El Mirador,' that big balcony high on the cliffs of the mountains that surround Mexico City from which the view is so marvelous. His purpose was not just to see the view, though. His investigation had revealed that Manolo and Julieta went often to El Mirador, literally 'the place to look from' on Saturdays, during their outings while they were dating. It was a favorite with lovers and artists. It is by the side of the old highway to Cuernavaca, that old winding devil of a road, with breath-taking mountain scenery filled with dangerous curves. Luis conjectured that maybe during one of their visits Manolo and Julieta had decided to make love and it had been then that she became pregnant. Luis wanted to see the place. As any good investigator knows, oftentimes you have to retrace all the movements of a person to understand his or her actions.

In any case, Luis had plenty of time to kill before meeting with Sabandija at 2:00 p.m. and 'El Mirador' was a marvelous place to go today.

He got to the junction where the toll highway goes to the left and the scenic route to the right. He turned right at the same time he up-shifted into fourth, then third, and accelerated. The toll highway was always full of traffic, but at this time of the day the winding old road was almost deserted. He passed a couple of trucks whose drivers probably wanted to save the toll and use it instead to buy some beer, and shifted back into fourth and fifth. The T-bird was doing sixty-five miles an hour with no apparent effort and the roar of the big exhausts in the middle of the wind was a delight to the ears of Luis.

That was when he first noticed a car behind him. His first reaction was to push the throttle in and to race a little with the other car, which seemed to be quickly gaining on him, but he remembered that his mechanic had warned him about the

Borrani wire-wheels. He had hit the right rear one while taking a tight turn and the mechanic asked him not to exert it before he had a chance to check it for inner damage. Wire-wheels are very beautiful but also very fragile.

Luis decided to take it easy, keep on going at sixty-five and allow the other driver to have his fun passing a sports car. It was an older Ford LTD, probably a '77 or '78, and it was approaching fast. When the other car was closer he could clearly see on the rearview mirror that five men were inside. He was still unconcerned, what the heck, they probably were workers car-pooling on their way to an afternoon shift at some of the factories near Cuernavaca who had decided to save the toll money.

But, looking on the rear-view mirror he realized that the car was coming way too fast and seemed headed directly to ram him from the back. Reacting with the speed of lightning, he shifted from fifth to third and even at sixty-five the big Interceptor engine made the Thunderbird jump forward like a deer. He looked on the mirror and could see that the other car was beginning to lose ground. He shifted to fourth, then fifth, and continued with the accelerator grounded. A nasty curve to the left was coming up on him and he had to up-shift again to take it. His tires screeched, badly tortured by the speed. He saw on the mirror the other car coming out of the curve almost sideways but the driver controlled it and kept on the pursuit. That man was a great driver, no question about it.

It is funny how the mind of a man reacts under pressure. The thoughts of Luis were fixed on the fact that he was carrying the Mexican money equivalent of over five thousand dollars in cash, Sabandija's reward, and that he was responsible for it. He did not know if the men were trying to rob him, to kill him, or if they were only having rough fun, he just felt that he had to protect Sabandija's cash.

Luis kept on driving at the highest possible speed. He could barely believe it, he was taking the curves at over sixty miles an hour and could not lose the other car even with the special suspension of his Thunderbird. It soon became obvious to him that the car following him was driven by an expert and probably as souped up as his own car. Otherwise there was no way they could be keeping up with his Thunderbird on this difficult winding highway.

They had now reached the part where the road climbs into the high cliffs and becomes a continuing succession of curves to the left and to the right. Luis was driving the Thunderbird between second and third gear virtually all the time now. He could see the other car beginning to lose some ground, but it was little that Luis was gaining. The road was still empty, but Luis shuddered at the idea of what would happen if he encountered a slow moving car or even worse, a truck.

Sure enough, just as he was thinking of that, he came out of a curve with his Pirelli tires screeching and he saw a truck in one of the curves ahead. It was a big one, fully loaded, with the cargo covered with a tarp and moving at a snail pace. He caught up with it in an instant and, with a curve coming up, he had no choice but to pass it blind. He moved to the left lane. The road there is extremely narrow, if there was another vehicle coming, he would crash head-on against it without remedy.

Luis was not a believer, he had been raised a Catholic but had drifted away from religion in the turmoil of his life. Now, remembering what Roberto had told him a few days before, he muttered: "God, my friend says you live and listen to your people. In Jesus name, let no one be coming from the opposite direction." He started passing the truck and could see the arm of the driver of the truck, madly waving at him to stop, not to pass. Obviously the man was seeing another oncoming vehicle. Luis had no choice, he was going way too fast. Almost resignedly, he upshifted to second and pushed the pedal as deep as he could and continued. Almost without being able to believe it, he was able to pass the truck and veered to the right just as the oncoming car, braking and honking wildly, brushed next to him. He looked on the mirror and could see that the car pursuing him was very close to the truck. Its driver would have to either brake really hard before crashing into the back of the truck or crash head on with the car that was coming down the mountain. In a fraction of a second, on the mirror he saw the arm and hand of the driver of the truck, signaling madly, as had signaled to him, not to pass. With horror, he saw that the pursuing car also disregarded the signals and moved to the left lane to pass the truck without reducing speed at all.

What followed was a scene out of Dante's inferno. The driver of the truck being passed moved as far right as he could, but there simply was not enough room for the two onrushing cars. Luis could not hear a screech of brakes, just the sickening noise of metal crashing. He started braking, but it still took him some time to stop the Thunderbird. Because of the road winding he could not manage to see the place where it had happened, but could still hear noises. He then quickly turned on the highway to return to the place of the crash. Coming out of the curve, he saw that the truck he had passed was unscathed by the accident, but the other two cars had gone over down the cliff with the inertia of the crash. The truck had stopped and the driver and his assistant had gotten out and crossed over to the other side of the road and now were staring with a look of horrified disbelief down the cliff where the two cars had caught fire on their way down below. Luis stopped the Thunderbird nose to nose with the truck and got out and crossed the highway to where the two men were standing.

"You crazy fools!" shouted the driver as soon as he saw him, probably believing that Luis and the other car had been involved in a race for the fun of it, "Now, look at what you've caused!"

"Calm down man," replied Luis, "These guys were chasing me, I'm a police officer," he said while he produced his badge. The badge said 'retired' with small letters on one side, but nobody noticed that.

"Oh... I'm sorry officer," said the other man, now with a respectful tone. "But you were saved by some power above, be sure of that."

"Why do you say that?" asked Luis.

"Well, you saw me waving at you to stop, didn't you?"

"Yes, but I had no choice but to try to pass you."

"I understand that, what I do not understand is how it could be that the car I saw so close when you were about to pass me, all of a sudden seemed to be farther back."

"What do you mean?" asked Luis intrigued.

"I saw the car coming on when you were about to pass me and I knew that you would not make it, isn't it true Pancho?" said the driver turning to ask his assistant.

"Sure thing," said the assistant, "I swear it officer, we saw the car just like this, really close," he said, motioning with his hands, "Then, the next instant, the car was not there, you passed, zoom, like this, and the next thing we know is that the car was farther away than it had seemed at first," he continued, still motioning with his hands in the usual Latin conversational manner.

"It is true officer," said the driver.

Luis was silent and pensive for a moment, then he said: "We better get out of here before there is another accident. Don't worry, I'll report the accident," said Luis, getting his cell phone out. He dialed the number of one of his old buddies in the Judicial Police, told him what had happened and asked him to call an ambulance and report it to the Highway Patrol. After that, he turned to the driver and his helper and said, "I've reported the accident and called for an ambulance, although I don't think anybody could survive this crash."

"Me neither," said the driver.

"No way," echoed Pancho, the assistant.

Luis got back in the Thunderbird but, before starting the engine, he bowed his head and said, "Lord Jesus, I don't know if I'm crazy but I believe you just saved my life as my friend Roberto said you have saved his life many times. As he says we need to do, I accept your free gift of salvation and turn over my life to you. Be my Lord as you have been my Savior."

Luis wondered how he could thank God for saving his life when at least six people had just been killed because of that. Then he remembered what Roberto had explained when Luis asked the same question during their conversation a few days before. Roberto had said, "God says in his Word, 'I will have mercy on whom I will have mercy,' it is not for us to know why He does what He does, just to give Him glory for what He does for us."

14

THE HACIENDA OF SAN GABRIEL

When Don Jose found out about the attacks on Roberto and on Luis, he was enraged. "Who does this motherfucker think he is? I'm going to kill him with my bare hands."

Luis was surprised at hearing him use such foul language. Although Don Jose's tactics could be forceful and he would not hesitate to use any legal means to get what he needed, Luis seriously doubted that Don Jose had ever ordered anybody killed, much less done it himself. It just showed how great his indignation was.

Luis said, "I believe I know who he is. All the tips I have received point out to the man I suspected from the beginning, Lupe Saldaña."

"Don Jose turned to the telephone and said, "What's the name? I'm calling the Attorney General and asking him to arrest the son of a bitch!"

"No, no, no, Don Jose, it would only escalate the problem. Let me try to talk with him and see if we can defuse the situation."

"I guess you're right, Luisito," the tone was more subdued, but Luis could see how upset he was. "Go ahead and try to meet with the man. Let's see if you can find a solution."

After the attack of the night before, Roberto had been pretty upset. He was a peaceful man who had no violent enemies. His practice had created him some animosities but not anything that would give rise to personal physical attacks. It did not feel nice to think that you could be the victim of an attack at any time. Roberto had lived through the Vietnam years where his physical integrity was always at risk. He had no desire whatsoever to relive those years. His fear had been made greater after finding out about the attack against Luis on the road to Cuernavaca.

He arrived at his office after lunch because he had gone directly to the federal court for a preliminary hearing on another case. As soon as he got to his office, Roberto called the Chief of the D.E.A. in Houston to get help with the investigations on Julieta's father. They had become friends at the time Roberto worked as an interpreter with the federal court.

After explaining to the Chief what he wanted, the Chief responded, "Sure, Roberto. We have an undercover man in Mexico who I'm positive will be able to help you. Let me get in touch with him and ask him to see you. He will probably need for you to travel to where he is in Mexico to speak with him. You would have no problem in doing that, would you?"

"Of course not. I'm ready to travel any time."

"Great, I'll call you soon. Just to be sure, give me the number of your cell phone, to be able to reach you at any time."

Shortly after Roberto finished speaking with the D.E.A. Chief, Dana announced that Luis was on line three.

"Hi, my friend, any news?" asked Roberto, eager to tell him of his conversation with the D.E.A. Chief.

"Great news. I just spoke with the man himself," said Luis.

"What man?"

"The man I suspect is Julieta's father."

"Wow," was Roberto's only answer.

"So, get ready and pack a bag with some golf clothes, because I am about to get on Don Jose's personal Learjet to fly to Houston and pick you up. We have an appointment with the man to play a game of golf tomorrow morning at 11:30."

"How did you manage that?" Roberto was really surprised.

"I had been suspecting that this guy is our man. After what happened to you and me, Don Jose was so upset that he wanted to have the guy arrested--"

"Not a good idea," interrupted Roberto.

"Of course not, I convinced him to let me try to speak with the man. Well, I just picked up the phone, dialed the number given to me by information in Morelia, where he lives, and after going through a secretary, the man picks up the phone."

"Just like that?"

"Just like that. So I tell him who I am and that an attorney who represents Don Jose wants to speak with him. He, of course, asks about what, and I tell him that about a property he might be interested on. This is because I discovered that at some point he had expressed some interest on a wonderful hacienda owned by Don Jose. The man responds, 'Good, if you can make it, I'll see both of you tomorrow at 11:30 at the San Rosendo Golf Club for a game of golf.' How do you like that?"

"Amazing. So I guess we're on our way?"

"You said this case has the highest priority for you. I took the liberty to say yes," said Luis.

"Absolutely. Where do you want me to go and at what time?"

Luis responded, "The pilots tell me that we can be landing in Houston by six this afternoon. So if you can be at a place called McGowen Aviation in the airport of Hobby at that time, we'll make it to the hacienda by ten."

"Does it have lights for a night landing?" asked Roberto.

"Of course, it even has a VOR to guide you in flying IFR, if there is low visibility," answered Luis, who was also a private pilot.

This time Roberto was really impressed. It is expensive enough to build a jet runway on a remote ranch, but to equip it with lights, omni-directional finder and landing systems to allow you to make an instrument approach, that is extraordinary.

Roberto got to the McGowen Aviation hangar just when the Learjet was taxing in, so as soon as the door opened, he was standing on the tarmac ready to board the plane. Luis already had a Stolichnaya and tonic in his hand and Roberto soon had his favorite Myers rum with Coke.

Once airborne, Roberto explained about his call to the D.E.A. Chief.

"Are you going to call him to let him know about the trip?" asked Luis after Roberto finished.

"No, I have world service. If he dials my cell phone number in Houston, I'll get the call wherever I am in the world... hopefully."

They both laughed.

Shortly before 9:30 p.m., the pilot announced through the PA that they were approaching their destination.

"I asked them to fly low over the hacienda," said Luis Gil, "It's on the approach path anyway, and I want you to see it from the air. I also asked the administrator, when I called to let him know that we would be staying here, to turn-on all the lights."

"Great." Roberto could now see down to one side, like a jewel on the dark setting of the mountains that surround it, the hacienda of San Gabriel shining in the clear night. It seemed to be very close to the long row of lights that indicated the presence of a jet runway down there. In fact, it was over a mile away, but from the air the hacienda and the runway looked as a round diamond and a baguette diamond on the giant setting of the black-gold ring formed by the mountains that surrounded the estate. It was a breathtaking view which both spent the rest of the time in silence enjoying, until the thrust reversers started braking the graceful Learjet on the runway.

When the plane came to a halt in front of a hangar, they stooped out of the plane and were greeted by two servants, both smartly dressed in tropical suits of white trousers and white hunter's jacket with short sleeves, who also got the luggage out.

Roberto, who loved warm weather, enjoyed the hot breeze and the sweet soft smell of the countryside while they walked to a Mercury Grand Marquis that was waiting for them, driven by another man in an identical white tropical suit.

Just then Roberto realized that they had never been inspected upon entering the country, and he asked, "What about our travel documents? I brought my passport."

"You don't need it, Don Jose is too important for the government to impose conditions on his guests," responded Luis with a joking tone.

They boarded the Grand Marquis and traveled to the hacienda, about 15 minute away on a gravel road. When they got to it, Roberto could see that it was a classic example of Spanish sixteenth century architecture. Monastic and austere, it reminded you of a miniature of El Escorial, the monastery-palace built by Philip II of Spain.

But, all sensation of austerity ceased as you crossed the big double doors that opened into an inner courtyard to the side of the estate. Inside, it was a feast of lights. The car stopped smack in the center of the courtyard. To the right, a series of wide steps could be seen leading up to what looked as a Roman temple, two stories high.

The Roman garden, as Roberto would later learn it was called, had been a warehouse in the times when the hacienda was a mining concern extracting silver to help make Mexico the main exporter of the metal in the world. After the restoration by Don Jose, the huge warehouse, the roof of which had caved-in, was turned into a roofless series of arches covered with marble and cobble stoned floors and called the Roman garden.

Another side of the courtyard where the car had stopped, looked into a long cobblestone road wide enough for a car to drive on it, and to the sides of it there were several gardens with different types of decoration.

"Twelve in all," informed Luis who was enjoying Roberto's amazement, "And there are twenty-two more gardens all over the place inside the wall."

15

LUPE SALDAÑA

After being taken to a palatial suite that the servants called the 'Phillip II suite,' Roberto took off his business suit and put on slacks and a sports shirt and crossed the living room of the suite to go to Luis's room.

A short time later they were both seated in the dining room. "This is the small one, the large one is only opened for banquets with lots of people," said Luis, while Roberto thought that this 'small' dining room was about five times the size of the formal dining room of his house in Houston.

The dinner was at a level you would expect in the most expensive restaurant of the world, served with a bottle of a marvelous red French Bordeaux wine.

The man waitering on them asked Luis if they wanted music and Luis answered yes. Soon after, a flow of beautiful light classical music started sounding from seemingly nowhere, but the sound quality was marvelous.

After dinner, they sat for a while in the salon adjoining the dining room where they were served brandy and offered cigars. The cigars were Davidoff. Roberto soon understood why Don Jose only smoked the excellent and mild Davidoff's.

"I could very easily get used to this kind of life," said Luis, putting into words exactly Roberto's sentiments.

After finishing the brandy and cigars they went out to the gardens and walked on the cobblestone path that Roberto had seen from the Grand Marquis, visiting occasionally one of the gardens to the right and left, while Luis, who had been there several times before, explained that it was the Japanese garden, or the roses garden, or the cactus garden, or whatever.

It was almost 1:30 in the morning when they retired.

They were supposed to meet Lupe Saldaña at 11:30 a.m. at the club. Luis, who seemed to be as prompt as Roberto, suggested that they should leave no later than ten, since it would be a good one-hour drive to the club and he wanted to be sure to be on time. "The man's paranoia is that he hates people who are not right on time," explained Luis about Saldaña.

"He must have a hard life in Mexico, the way most Mexicans are," answered Roberto, who being Mexican-born felt free to criticize.

The drive to the country club was uneventful. The gravel road, which as Roberto had imagined the night before continued past the hacienda to a small town some twenty miles away, was in good shape although a little dusty, but the excellent suspension and air conditioning of the Mercury Grand Marquis made it almost unnoticeable. Upon leaving the small town, they got on a well-paved two-lane highway, which they followed for about forty minutes before getting to the club.

When they had the club in sight, Luis, who was sitting in the rear, leaned over to Roberto, sitting on the passenger side of the front bench and told him: "Roberto, did I tell you how Saldaña is known around here?"

"No."

"As the Mexican Godfather."

"Great, I appreciate it very much that you give me this piece of information just right now, shortly before we are to confront the man with an accusation of being a drug trafficker and just when we will be trying to force out of him a confession of having set-up a trap for Manolo."

Luis just sat back again, with a big, broad grin on his face.

They walked into the club and intercepted an employee to ask him if he knew Lupe Saldaña. "Don Lupe? Of course, he is that gentleman sitting at the table next to the window," he responded pointing. Luis and Roberto followed the pointed hand.

Saldaña did not fit at all the mental image that Roberto had made of him. He had imagined a coarse, uneducated man surrounded by bodyguards with submachine-guns who would give them a pat-down before allowing them to even approach their boss. What he saw was an immaculately dressed man, with the distinguished look of a professional. He was wearing a golf outfit that from the golf cap, resting on the table next to him, to the golf shoes was exactly the same peach color. He was sitting at a table relaxing and gazing out into the green spaces of the golf grounds while he smoked a cigarette and sipped at a drink that could be a screwdriver or orange juice, Roberto did not know which.

Saldaña stood up when he saw Luis approaching. He was almost as tall as Luis Gil, of a slim build but strong, with black hair graying on the temples and a strong, square jaw that gave him a definite air of determination. To Roberto, he looked remarkably like the character of Anthony Quinn in the 'Greek Tycoon.' Roberto could see that he was wearing an ultra-flat gold watch with a black leather strap. Roberto could not see the brand of the watch but he was certain that it was expensive without being showy.

Luis extended his hand and said, "Mr. Saldaña."

Saldaña's voice was deep and a little hoarse when he spoke, "You must be Commander Gil?"

"Yes sir, nice to meet you."

It did not escape Roberto's attention that Luis had not used the respectful 'Don' in addressing him. Saldaña turned to Roberto and said, "And you must be counselor Duran, right?"

"Yes, Mr. Saldaña, nice to meet you," said Roberto following Luis's cue.

Saldaña asked them if they cared for orange juice (so it had been orange juice after all) or coffee and they both asked for coffee and sat down while Saldaña ordered it from one of the waiters. Roberto could not see anybody around him that looked like a bodyguard and he could not help but think that Don Jose's security seemed to be tighter than Saldaña's.

Their conversation was the typical chat between educated Mexicans, no mention of business, only the weather, how beautiful the club was, and the like. Roberto knew that Mexican courtesy demanded that it was not until Saldaña decided to speak about business that they could do so. After a short while, Saldaña suggested that his guests should change into golf clothes. So he took them to the dressing room to choose the golf clubs and shoes they preferred.

Luis and Roberto changed and joined Saldaña out in the pro shop, where he gave them their green fee tickets already paid for and asked them for their handicap. Saldaña was much better player than the other two, so they made the necessary adjustments to keep the score even and went out to tee number one.

Luis started with a good solid drive, Roberto followed with his usual trustworthy but short drive and Saldaña teed off with a marvelous drive that almost put him on the green. They continued the game with Saldaña consistently outplaying both of them, but with the score keeping more or less even thanks to the handicap he had given them. Roberto had to confess to himself that he was enjoying the game and the conversation with this man. Saldaña demonstrated an ample culture and refinement that were surprising in a man of his trade, but evident nevertheless.

It was not until they teed off number five that Saldaña opened the conversation about business. He was walking next to Roberto when he suddenly said, "Counselor, I understand Don Jose sent you gentlemen to make some kind of proposition?" he said while they walked on to the fairway.

"Yes, Mr. Saldaña, I am an attorney who practices in Houston and—"

"In Houston?" asked Saldaña with surprise.

"Yes, sir, in Houston. Are you surprised?"

"Well you speak Spanish as a Mexican and I had understood that you represented Don Jose?"

"Actually sir, I represent Manolo, Don Jose's grandson, and, yes, I was born and raised in Mexico City, only that I now practice in Houston."

"I see. So, you represent Manolo. What business is the young man in, nowadays?"

Roberto was well aware that in a marvelous feat of public relations, Don Jose had managed to keep any mention of Manolo's troubles off the Mexican media, where it would eventually become big news. In Houston, the media did not even seem to notice that a wealthy Mexican had been arrested. It was only logical, American media only paid attention to powerful current or former politicians from Latin America who had already been in the news in their own countries. For them, Manolo was a non-story. Roberto tried to detect any irony in Saldaña's question but there seemed to be none, he responded, "Well, it's a long story," and he started a narrative of what had happened.

They got to number seven before Roberto finished telling

Saldaña about Manolo's arrest. All the while Roberto had his
sensors alert trying to detect anything in Saldaña that would
show he knew about the matter. But Saldaña would only nod or
make some comment of surprise with no indication that he knew
anything at all. Either he was a fantastic poker player or he really
didn't know a thing.

Roberto knew that the hard part would be to tell Saldaña
about what Luis suspected as the real reason for their visit to
him. How do you tell someone that you suspect he set a trap for
your client as revenge for the death of his daughter without alien-
ating him?

Before Roberto could continue, Saldaña said "So, I imagine
that the reason you came to see me is because you want my help
with respect to information about the drugs."

"Yes sir. That is exactly what we want."

"And how, may I ask, do you want me to help?"

"Well Mr. Saldaña," said Roberto tentatively, "Commander
Gil suggested that you might know something."

"No, I don't," said Saldaña pensively, as almost to himself,
while he teed off number eight with another perfect drive,
"Which is strange because there is little in this business that I do
not know about," he continued.

Roberto sighed with relief, at least the subject was now in the
open. Saldaña was accepting that he was in the drug-dealing
business. That simplified things, so he said, "Frankly sir, my idea
was that you, maybe... that it was your group that placed the
cocaine in Manolo's bags, as revenge."

He said it after Luis finished his drive. Saldaña, who was
beginning to walk on the fairway, stopped liked if he had hit an
invisible wall. "Why on earth would I do that?" he asked, and
turned around with a note of evident anger in his voice.

Luis, who had been following the conversation, came to
Roberto's rescue explaining that he was the one that had come up
with the idea.

Saldaña resumed his walking forward fast, followed by Roberto and by Luis, who was still trying to calm him down. Halfway from the tee to the green, he stopped and Luis stopped to his left, almost facing him, while Roberto caught up with them to stand between the two of them, and to one side. Luis kept on speaking while Saldaña brought out an elegant gold cigarette case from his back left trouser pocket and a matching Dunhill lighter from his front right pocket and produced a cigarette. His hands were a little shaky from the anger and the cigarette fell to the ground, instinctively Roberto bent over to pick it up at the same time Saldaña was bending over.

Exactly when bending down, Roberto heard a loud shot that echoed in the open spaces of the golf course. It was a single shot, but Roberto hit the ground immediately while he saw Saldaña and Luis throwing themselves down too.

Luis was not carrying the 9 millimeters Beretta at this time, it was too big to conceal, but Roberto saw that Luis pulled out a .38 caliber Smith & Wesson airweight revolver without a hammer from the ankle holster. At the same time he looked back to see the three caddies. Roberto had felt, more than seen, that the caddies had taken a little longer to duck than they three had, but now he could see that Saldaña's caddie was next to the golf bag, which seemed to have opened in half, and was fumbling with what looked like a sawed-off shotgun that he was trying to get out of the bag.

Then they heard a short burst of what sounded like a .225 caliber M-16 followed by another burst, this time of a larger caliber that seemed as of an AK-47 Kalachnikoff assault rifle. Saldaña's caddie had gotten back on his feet and fired the two shots of the shotgun. It was a reflex reaction, there was no possibility whatsoever he would hit anything. The single shot had been fired by a high-power rifle, probably from pretty far away.

Luis, far more controlled, had the little gun in his hand but didn't fire it. Saldaña also had a gun in his hand, Roberto could see that it was a small caliber automatic, probably a .25, but he did not fire it either.

The whole episode lasted less than thirty seconds and an odd silence ensued. Roberto was very familiar with the silence. People seem to think that being in combat is to be constantly in action, but Roberto remembered it as hours of boredom interspersed with a few seconds of sheer panic. Just as now, nobody moves after an exchange of fire, until one by one men start getting up to evaluate the situation. The same thing happened now.

The first one to get up was Saldaña, his caddie, who had ducked after jerking off the two shots, tried to pull him down but Saldaña dismissed him with a motion of the hand. Then Roberto and Luis stood up and two caddies followed, Saldaña's and Luis's. 'Where is my caddie,' thought Roberto, just as he looked around and saw the man lying face down towards the tee. 'Strange' -he thought-, everybody had hit the ground facing the green from where the shot had come. Then, Roberto saw the pool of blood that was already forming next to the man's head. Everyone seemed to notice it at the same time and they all walked slowly to the man, as if afraid of discovering what they already knew.

Roberto, perhaps because it was his caddie, was the one who turned the man over, just to move back horrified while the body slumped back to lie on his back, the grotesque third eye of a bullet-hole slightly to the right of his forehead, as if staring at Roberto.

They all stood there, just looking at the man, while several men armed with M-16s and goat-corns, as the Kalachnikoff assault rifles are popularly called in Mexico, approached them. Saldaña went towards them and started talking to them. They were probably reporting and asking for instructions. Roberto thought that it was funny that he had not noticed any security at all before.

"Roberto, you know something?" said Luis standing next to him.

"What?"

"They were not trying to get Mr. Saldaña, nor me. That bullet was meant for you."

Roberto could feel the cold sweat streaming down his armpits with the realization. Luis had to be right, his caddie had been the exact same height as Roberto and had been standing exactly to his back when he bent over to pick up Saldaña's cigarette.

Roberto did not say a thing but in a reflex movement he touched his forehead, as if feeling an invisible bullet-hole. He felt terribly sorry for the man killed and would do anything in his power to see that the man's family be provided for, but could not help but feel that the Lord had saved him once more. Roberto muttered to himself, "Thank you Lord."

16

THE UNDERCOVER MAN

Their golf match ended abruptly. No one had any desire to continue after what happened. Saldaña asked them if they wanted to have a cup of brandy and both Luis and Roberto earnestly answered yes. Once in the luxuriously appointed bar, Saldaña ordered a bottle of Courvoisier and three cognac goblets.

After seating, Saldaña abruptly addressed Roberto, "Now, Counselor, why on earth did you think I would set up such an elaborate trap for Manolo, placing cocaine in his bags and then tipping off Customs in the United States?"

It was Luis who answered, "As I was telling you before this incident, it was me who thought you might have."

"Why?" asked Saldaña simply.

"Because, Manolo may have caused the suicide of your daughter, Julieta," said Luis. Roberto held his breath, expecting an outburst of anger or of pain from the man.

There was no need. Saldaña, just smiled openly and said, "My dear Commander Gil, I have no children. My only marriage ended in divorce many years ago and I never had any children. So, you see, Manolo could not have caused the suicide of any daughter of mine. Of course, your theory is sound. Find the man who was the father of the girl and you probably find the man who placed the cocaine in Manolo's bags."

Roberto felt relieved. He did not understand why, but he liked Saldaña. On the other hand, he also felt disappointed. This was just a dead end. They were no closer to finding the answer to the riddle than they had been at the beginning.

Luis must have felt the same because he said with a sigh, "So you are not our man?"

"No, I'm not. But whoever is, must be pretty upset at you guys. That shot was aimed at Mr. Duran."

"Yes, that is what I believe also," said Luis. Roberto just nodded.

"Well, for the time being, let's forget about conspiracies and enjoy our Cognacs, the answer may come to you two sooner than you expect," said Saldaña and Roberto wondered why he had said it.

A couple of hours later, the president of the club approached the table to ask if everything was well and to offer apologies and assurances that they did not need to worry about anything. The club would take care of everything, arrange the burial of the man and make arrangements with the police to quiet things down. Roberto did not know about the other two, but he personally felt relieved by those words. He did not need a big mess in his hands with the Mexican police.

They all thanked the man, who before leaving said, "And, the bottle of Courvoisier is on the house."

By the time they parted company, they were all on a first name basis. There is no better way to create rapport between men than to drink together a bottle of fine Cognac.

After saying good-bye to Saldaña, Luis and Roberto boarded the Mercury Grand Marquis on the porch of the club for the trip back to the hacienda. Luis sat on the front bench seat this time because Roberto, who was feeling slightly drowsy with the Cognac, wanted to take a nap in the back seat.

They had been on the road for about fifteen minutes and Roberto had already fallen asleep when he was awakened by the vibration of his cell phone in the left pocket of his trousers. On the front bench, the driver and Luis did not even notice that the small telephone had rang. Roberto removed it from his pocket and answered it, still drowsy.

"Roberto Duran?"

"Roberto?" It was the voice of the Chief of the Houston District Office of the D.E.A.

"Hi, Bill," answered Roberto wide-awake now.

"I'm sorry, I think I woke you up," said the Chief apologetically.

"I was just taking a short nap. What's up?"

"I got in touch with our undercover man down there. He is ready to see you tomorrow at 10:00 a.m., if you can make it."

"I'll try, I'm here in the middle of nowhere at the border of the states of Jalisco and Michoacan in the Republic of Mexico. But I believe I would be able to travel anywhere on short notice," responded Roberto, remembering the Learjet and Don Jose's instructions to use it to move as freely as Luis and he wanted.

"Great. My man tells me that there is this golf club that is supposed to be pretty well known down there. It is near Morelia, where he lives. The name is San Rosendo. Do you have an idea of how far away it is from where you are?"

"Yes. It's about fifteen minutes away," responded Roberto, amazed at the coincidence that the meeting place would be right where they had just been.

"Is that right?" said the Chief.

"Absolutely, I have just been playing golf there. A game that was interrupted by someone shooting at me."

"Shooting at you?" asked the Chief with surprise.

"Yes. I'll tell you all about it once I'm back. For now, I will be at San Rosendo tomorrow at 10:00 sharp," said Roberto.

"Good. I'll let my undercover man know. Call me when you're back, this case you are working on seems fun," said the Chief, with a festive tone.

"You bet, lots of fun. Thanks Chief. I'll see you soon."

"Bye, Roberto."

Luis had turned around on the seat. He had noticed the call after Roberto answered and overheard the conversation, so he was pretty curious. He was aware that Roberto was expecting a call from the Houston D.E.A. Chief.

"Any news?" asked Luis.

Roberto explained and Luis was as amazed as Roberto by the coincidence. Saldaña had agreed with Roberto and Luis that he would try to find out as much as he could about Manolo's situation. With their fears allayed by the cognac and being that the three had really enjoyed their company together, they had agreed to meet the following morning at 11:00 to finish that game of golf that had been interrupted.

Luis said, "Well, the situation is this, we have a meeting at 10 a.m. with an undercover drug agent, and another at 11 a.m. with one of the most powerful drug barons in Mexico. Do you think it's a good idea?"

Roberto laughed, "No, I don't, but can you think of anything we can do?"

"I guess what we have to do is to be extremely prompt for both our appointments," said Luis.

The next morning Luis and Roberto were in the office of the San Rosendo Country Club at exactly 9:45 a.m.

"This guy better not be late. You know what a nut for punctuality Saldaña is," said Luis.

"I just hope the man from the D.E.A. is as prompt as Saldaña," replied Roberto.

The conference room they were in had a glass wall covered with a very light drape that allowed one to see through and distinguish what was happening outside the room. Roberto and Luis were sipping at a cup of coffee when someone walked into the office area next to the conference room. They both looked into that direction and their reaction was to look at each other startled and annoyed. It was Lupe Saldaña, and he was now walking toward the door of the conference room after saying something to the two secretaries seated outside. He was the last person they wanted to see at that time.

Roberto glanced at his watch and said, "Shit! He's early."

"What do we do?" asked Luis, equally unnerved.

They did not have time to say or do anything more. The door opened and Lupe Saldaña walked in. "Roberto, Luis," he said, shaking the hands of both. "You seem surprised to see me."

"Well... eh... yes, Lupe," said Roberto. "Actually, yes, we are surprised. We have another matter to take care of. Were we not supposed to meet until eleven?"

"Nope," replied Lupe.

"No?" asked Roberto, "At what time then?"

"I meant to say that, yes, we were indeed supposed to meet at eleven," replied Lupe. "But you do not have any other matter to take care of, I am the man your friend from Houston said you would be meeting with at ten."

The enormity of Lupe's statement hit both Roberto and Luis hard. They both remained for a few seconds staring at Lupe. Lupe, who was obviously enjoying the moment, asked innocently, "What, gentlemen, do you really believe everything is what it seems to be?"

Roberto recovered enough to say, "Lupe, this is so strange that--"

"Let me interrupt you right there, my friend," he said, putting his finger across his lips. "Why don't we all change into golf clothes and go out to the course. We will have time and opportunity to chat once we start playing."

They changed into sports clothes and golf shoes and once on the open field and while they played their eighteen holes, Lupe explained to both of them his whole story. Nobody interrupted, Roberto and Luis were fascinated by what they heard. The caddies were obviously hand-picked by Lupe and there was no problem to talk in front of them.

It was an extraordinary story. Jose Guadalupe Saldaña, which was his whole name, had been born 77 years before in San Diego, California, the third son to a sergeant in the United States Army stationed near the border between Mexico and California. His father was of Mexican descent and insisted that his son should learn fluent Spanish, so Lupe attended an American school in the morning and a Mexican school in the evening.

By the time he finished High School in the United States, he had also finished Preparatory School in Mexico and was ready to attend a professional school in Mexico or four more years attending college in the U.S. and then a professional school, if he wanted to continue his studies in America. Lupe opted for Mexico. He enrolled in the School of Engineering of the Monterrey Institute of Technology, the most prestigious engineering school in the Republic of Mexico. He was in his first year there when Pearl Harbor was attacked and the United States became embroiled in World War II. Immediately he crossed back to the United States and volunteered for the Army. He was underage, but recruiters could easily be convinced that one was 18 at the beginning of the war.

Lupe trained to be a paratrooper and was sent to Europe with the 82nd Airborne Division. He saw action in several battles with the famous division. He was injured during the German counteroffensive at the Bois des Ardennes, the famous battle of the

Bulge, and received a purple heart for it together with many other decorations.

After the war, he returned to Monterrey to continue his studies. Three years later, he got his degree with honors in civil engineering. He had met a girl from Monterrey in his last year in the Institute of Technology and fell in love with her. After a short courtship, they got married. Next, he got a job with a big construction firm in Mexico City. Once in Mexico City, he rented a comfortable apartment in a high rise in the Polanco area. It was an upper class subdivision and Lupe and his wife settled there to live a typical bourgeois life.

But fate had other plans. During the first year of their marriage, Lupe was working extra time to make ends meet and advance in his profession. His beautiful young bride was getting bored. Evil sent a young man from Monterrey who had dated the girl before Lupe met her, was still unmarried and went to live in the same apartment building as Lupe and his young wife. Soon after, she was having an affaire with her former date. Lupe discovered it almost by accident and his fury knew no limit.

One night, he waited for the man to arrive and confronted him. The other man, out of sheer stupidity or foolhardy bragging, tried to punch him rather than trying to calm him down. They exchanged a few blows, but the other man was no match whatsoever for a crack paratrooper. Lupe killed him, unintentionally but enraged, with his bare hands.

Obviously he had to leave Mexico. He fled back to the United States, but even there, he was fearful that the authorities would be after him, so he never contacted his family. Since he had to make a living and did not want to use his degree in engineering, he used his military training instead and mixed with the underworld. Soon, he had acquired a reputation as a triggerman and enforcer. He started making much more money than he could have made by working honestly and, in his disappointment and disillusion, he became a cynic in the matters of life. It was the time of the Korean War and soon he started dealing in stolen goods from the U.S. Army.

When the Korean war ended, he was wealthy. He decided to go back to Mexico under an assumed identity. Once in Mexico, he found out that the Mexican Police had ruled the death of the other man accidental and that he was not even a wanted man. Learning that, he confronted the woman who was still officially his wife and got a divorce from her. There had been no children in the marriage, so it was a clean break.

With his money and underworld connections, Lupe started dealing with smuggled electronic goods into Mexico. The Mexican government, trying to help its budding industry, had restricted the importation of electronic goods into Mexico so that domestic production could take off. The consequences were that smuggling of electronics became a fantastic business.

Before long, Lupe owned five DC-3s with American registration numbers that flew regularly between San Diego and the State of Michoacan where he established his base, stuffed with electronic smuggled goods. The beginning of the sixties brought tighter border controls and higher import duties for electronics in Mexico, so his business prospered.

At the same time, the use of marihuana had spread enormously in the United States, so the enterprising mind of Lupe devised a system by which he brought electronics into Mexico and on the same airplane he smuggled marihuana back into the United States.

He would have continued until caught by law enforcement authorities or killed by some competitor, had it not been because God had other plans for him. After he returned to Mexico, he had gotten in touch with his family once again. It was early in the decade of the great revivals in California and his father had become a born-again Christian and started asking his son to attend the services with him. Lupe was in very good terms with his father, whom he loved and respected. The father suspected that the business of the son might not be totally within the bounds of the law and expressed his concern several times, but Lupe always calmed him down saying that his import-export business was totally legitimate in the United States, that it was into Mexico that he smuggled goods. The explanation was not totally satisfactory for the father who kept on insisting upon Lupe to come to one of the non-denominational services that he attended.

Lupe did not feel much inclination toward spiritual things, but his father was by now old and Lupe wanted to make him happy, so he gave in and went to his father's church. He had made up his mind that he would go a few times and then tell his father that he had tried it but was really not interested.

But the Spirit of the Lord touched his heart during that first service and he stood up at the time of the altar call. Almost without believing what he was doing, he walked to the front of the temple, prayed the sinner's prayer and turned his life over to Jesus. He immediately felt cleansing in his life. His many sins were washed away in the blood of the Lamb and he decided to change his lifestyle.

At first he decided to sell the airplanes and abandon the unlawful business. Some time before he had bought a ranch in Michoacan, near San Rosendo, and had started planting orchards where he produced peaches and other fruits, so he decided he would go live there. But again, the Lord had different plans for him. When he advertised to sell the airplanes, several shady characters came to him showing interest in buying the whole fleet, by now of eight planes.

Lupe suspected all of them were smugglers but he was still worldly enough not to care too much. One of them started asking probing questions on why Lupe was selling the planes. Lupe simply answered that business was not as good going into Mexico as it used to be, 'too much surveillance from the Mexican authorities,' he said. The other man smiled understandingly and then made a business proposition. Wouldn't Lupe like the idea of associating with him? Lupe responded that he was really not interested, but the other man kept on insisting and Lupe finally asked for details. The bottom line was that the other man had sources of supply of cocaine in Colombia and he wanted the fleet to bring it into the United States. Lupe was still not extremely full of scruples against smuggling, but electronic goods and even marihuana were one thing, cocaine was another. After his recent conversion and with the memories he still kept of a couple of his wartime buddies hooked on morphine, he decided to contact a friend of his father who worked for the predecessor of the Drug Enforcement Administration and report to him what the man was proposing.

The man from the D.E.A.'s predecessor was extremely interested. He asked Lupe to pretend to go along with the plan and set a trap for the traffickers. There was an added incentive, the man from D.E.A. said, Lupe could collect a good amount of money at the end of the case if it resulted in the seizure of a sizable amount of drugs or money or the indictment of a few defendants. Lupe was not interested in the money, he had enough, but on the other hand he felt he had a debt to society that he should repay, so he said yes.

His work was so efficient and his connections with the underworld so credible, that a couple of years later, the D.E.A. offered him a job and brought him onboard as a Special Agent. By then Lupe had discovered that he loved to catch crooks, so he accepted and became the top D.E.A. contact in Mexico while posing as a drug baron.

17

THE TERRORIST

"Unbelievable," said Roberto, while Luis assented with his head. They had almost finished playing the golf course. While they walked to the eighteenth tee, Roberto continued, "So all this time, Lupe, you have been working as an undercover agent?"

"That's right," replied Lupe, who had enjoyed telling these friends about his whole story. In the dangerous and elusive world of undercover operations it is a great relaxation to be able to tell someone you can trust about who you really are. Besides, he enjoyed the surprise of his two new friends, they had not known each other for long but there was already a bond forming between the three.

They got to the eighteenth hole and prepared to tee-off. At the start, they had decided they would score by hole, Lupe would give Roberto and Luis one stroke each in all par-4 and par-5 holes. They were even now after seventeen holes. Each of them had won five holes, and two holes had ended even. The last hole would decide the whole game.

Eighteen was a par 5, and a mischievous one. The fairway

made a turn to the right and the green was relatively close to the tee, but any attempt to fly over the out-of-bounds area would be thwarted by three big trees on the right side of the fairway. You had to play straight onto the fairway. The wind was blowing pretty hard at a 45-degree angle from the right. The caddy handed Roberto his driver. Roberto looked at it thoughtfully and then asked for his 3 wood.

"Not a good choice, Roberto, too much wind," commented Lupe.

"Lupe's right," added Luis.

"I know," said Roberto, "But I am very bad with the driver, I feel a lot more comfortable with a 3 wood." He took his 3 wood, which he had used to tee-off on each of the five holes he had won so far. Roberto felt his tension building up while his two friends looked on him as he aligned himself toward the center of the fairway and hit the ball. His tense muscles hindered the blow and the club head struck too low on the ball which went very high in the air, the wind caught the ball and sent it out-of-bounds to the right.

His two friends commented on Roberto's bad luck, but were not exactly in mourning over it. It was a friendly game, but as usual with high-powered individuals, not devoid of competition. Lupe went next and put a marvelous drive to the center of the fairway, perfect for a second shot directly to the green. Luis hit an extraordinarily solid drive that went over Lupe's ball and almost out-of-bounds to the left where the fairway turns to the right, but stopped short of leaving the fairway.

Roberto had a pretty good idea where his ball was and found it without difficulty. His caddie suggested using a 5 iron through a small opening to the green while Roberto evaluated the situation. Right in front of him were the three very large and bushy trees whose branches went down all the way almost to the ground. The green was immediately behind the trees. Roberto knew that it would have to be a very good shot to get through the obstacles. Knowing that he was not very good at aiming a golf ball, he turned to his caddie and said, "Give me an 8 iron."

"An 8 iron sir! You'll never make it; if you get the ball over the trees, you will overshoot the green."

"Give it to me anyway," insisted Roberto with a conciliatory tone.

The caddie handed him his 8 iron while he muttered something that Roberto could not make out. Probably that Roberto was out of his mind. But Roberto had recognized that the wind direction was blowing exactly opposite to where he wanted to send his ball, so he made his swing and this time hit precisely where he wanted. The ball went high into the air and for a split second it seemed as if it was going to badly overshoot the green, just then, a gust of wind stopped the ball in mid-air and made it drop almost straight down on the green to roll softly to less than one foot from the hole.

"You lucky son of a gun," yelled Luis from far away, while Roberto grinned, now he had a chance to beat them. Even with the two-stroke penalty for out-of-bounds, he would end with the par for the hole, minus one for the handicap, he could make the hole in four. His two friendly opponents were now under stress.

Lupe hit a good stroke but was short of the green. Luis badly overshot the green. In his third stroke, Luis, obviously nervous, sent the ball all the way back to the other side of the green. Lupe got on the green in his third stroke. Finally, they both where on the green, Luis in four, Lupe in three, but they were both pretty far from the hole. Roberto could not wait any longer and with a soft sweep he sank his ball. By the time both Luis and Lupe were in, the adjusted score for the hole was, Roberto four, Lupe five and Luis five. Against all odds, Roberto had won.

"Son of a gun, were you lucky or do you actually play a lot better than you made us believe?" asked Luis.

"Just lucky," replied Roberto.

"No, I don't believe you were lucky, not with this shot anyway," said Lupe admiringly, "You obviously calculated the wind velocity and made a marvelous play."

"Lupe's right," said Luis, with a teasing tone, "No question you attorneys are devious characters, while we law enforcement officers are honest and straightforward. Isn't that true Lupe?"

"Sure is. Never trust an attorney," said Lupe with a straight face, "You know how you can tell when an attorney is lying? When his lips are moving. Let's go to the nineteenth hole, I need a Cognac."

Back in the clubhouse's bar, with a bottle of Courvoisier in front of them, after Luis and Lupe teased Roberto for a while, they went on to serious business.

Luis said, "We are back to square one. Lupe, can you help us determine who is the mysterious father of Julieta?"

"I must tell you that as soon as the Houston Chief called me, my people began to investigate what I believe to be the more promising lead."

"What is that?" asked Roberto.

"We have known for years that there is a very powerful drug lord who poses as a prominent businessman, although we have never been able to determine who he is," responded Lupe.

"That is consistent with what the triggerman told me," said Luis, and explained to Lupe the strange late night encounter near Garibaldi Square.

"Yes, that is what we know also. The only thing we know for sure is that he changes personality periodically. Every time we feel he have identified him, he changes identity. We decided to give him the code name of 'M' and, one way or another, he found out about it and it seems that he has adopted it."

"'M'?" asked Roberto.

"Yes. He even had the gall to send us an e-mail signed 'M' once."

"An e-mail is essentially very traceable, isn't it?" asked Roberto.

"Not this one," said Lupe, "We traced it back to the Philippines, to an address that never existed. So you see, the man is elusive."

"Sure is," said Luis. "Do you think he is our man?"

"Might be. There is no way to know if he has any family without knowing his identity," said Lupe.

"That's true," responded Roberto. "Luis, how about contacting the mother of the girl, she knows for sure who the father is."

Two days later, back in Houston, Roberto was sitting at his Lopez-Morton desk, looking pensively out the large window to his left into the Houston skyline while he listened to the sound of one of Mozart's French horn concertos very softly in the background. Lupe Saldaña had agreed to continue investigating and advise them of any lead. Luis promised to speak with the mother of Julieta and find out about the father of the girl, yet Roberto knew that the trial was set for the following month and he really did not have a clear strategy for getting Manolo acquitted.

The intercom buzzed and Roberto mechanically looked at his watch. It was 10:30 sharp, 'Prompt as usual,' thought Roberto. He had an appointment with Bobby Cavazos, his free-lance investigator, to discuss about Manolo's case. "Yes," he said into the intercom.

"Mr. Cavazos to see you, Mr. Duran," responded Ginny, his receptionist.

"Thank you Ginny, send him in." He stood up and walked to

the door and opened it in time to see the rubicund figure of Cavazos walking down the hall. "Nice to see you, Bobby," he said, "It's always good to see someone smile when you are depressed."

Bobby Cavazos looked exactly the opposite of how one imagines a private investigator to look. He was short, seemingly overweight, with a perennial smile on his kindly face and the nicest personality you can imagine. But Roberto felt sorry for those who might try to abuse this very nice individual. Bobby had a core of the hardest steel. He was a fourth degree black belt in Karate and a small-guns expert who had proven deadly when he worked for the Houston SWAT team.

"I don't see how someone like you can be depressed, boss," responded Cavazos, "You are good looking, rich, famous and smart," he finished with a grin.

"This time you missed the fact that I also smell nice, Bobby," said Roberto, picking up the joke, while he invited Cavazos in and asked him to sit in front the big desk. "Now, Bobby, start telling the truth. What do we have in the Gomez-Iglesias case."

"Something extremely important, boss," responded Cavazos becoming serious, "I got a copy of the lab analysis from Dallas, the total weight of the cocaine was sixty pounds."

"I know, I talked to Block and he told me about the sixty pounds, which is terrible, the possible punishment is so much more severe, but what exactly is so important?"

"Well, one of the things that Customs officers do with incoming baggage is to weigh it. If it is excessively heavy, they will invariably refer it to secondary. With what Manolo had in the bags, the weight was more than three times that of a normal bag, so the officers would have referred it for inspection regardless of any tip. Whoever framed Manolo wanted to be sure that he would get caught."

"I see. That is interesting, and probably will help for a defense."

"That's not all, boss, that's not even the most interesting part," said Cavazos, "Are you firmly seated?"

"Yes, I am," responded Roberto with a smile, "What else do you have for me Bobby?"

"The cocaine was only 30% pure. You know what that means, right?" said Cavazos.

"Pheeeww," went Roberto. Of course he knew what it meant. Normally, the 'mules', as the cocaine carriers are called, would bring substance that was over 90% pure. The reason being that on the streets cocaine is sold at a purity of about 30%. That level is achieved by 'cutting' the cocaine down, that is, adding other chemicals to make more volume and sell more of it. That way the mules bring in, say 10 kilos. Once in the United States, the cocaine is cut and with that process you get 40 kilos to sell on the streets. It would be totally insane for a trafficker to risk it bringing cocaine that could not be cut.

"That may be the break we have been looking for," said Roberto.

"Also, as you already know, the bags seized at the airport were not genuine Louis Vuitton," said Bobby.

"Yes, just as that Mexican informant told Luis. The problem is that it does not help me much because the jury might believe that Manolo bought counterfeit bags instead of the genuine ones," replied Roberto, "Although you and I know that Manolo would never buy a counterfeit bag."

"True," said Booby. "Anyway, I have some more good news," continued Cavazos, pulling some documents out of his briefcase and putting them on top of Roberto's desk, "Here you have the statements in writing of two passengers who were traveling with Manolo in the Aeromexico flight in which he arrived. Both are unrelated to each other, both statements were taken separately, and both agree that Manolo was surrounded by a group of tough-looking men who jumped on him the minute the Customs inspector cut the lining of the first bag. They both agree further that the agents were pretty rough on the kid. Furthermore, they both are willing, ready and able to give a deposition and even to testify at trial. They were really pretty shocked by the actions of the law enforcement officers."

"Bobby, as it so often happens, you have made my day," said Roberto.

18

CESAR

Luis parked his '57 Thunderbird near Mrs. Julieta Velasco's house on Gabriel Mancera street. It had not been as difficult as Luis had originally thought it would be to get the appointment. Introducing himself as 'Comandante Gil,' Luis conveyed the idea that this was an official investigation and Mrs. Velasco, a little surprised, agreed to meet with him.

He rang the bell after making the observation that the house was very well appointed. The maid came out and Luis stated that Mrs. Velasco was waiting for him at seven. The maid clearly had received instructions. Without hesitation, she opened the gate and preceded him to a very elegant living room. It was obvious that the lady of the house had good taste and the means to satisfy it. The maid asked him to take a seat which Luis did, just to get up almost immediately because he saw Mrs. Velasco coming down the stairs.

She was a woman of exceptional beauty, tall, about 5'8" and of a slim build. She seemed to be no older than late thirties. Her face was a very nice oval with high cheekbones, a very sweet mouth and a beautiful complexion. The eyes were strikingly green framed by her beautiful light brown hair. She was pale and had large purple shadows under her beautiful eyes. It was apparent that she had suffered very much. Luis assumed that it had to be for the death of her only child, but his detective mind also conjectured that maybe that mysterious man who fathered Julieta was also partially responsible for it.

"Commander Gil?" she said extending her hand and with a sad but welcoming smile on her beautiful face.

"Yes, Mrs. Velasco, sorry to have to inconvenience you," responded Luis, with the courtesy that is always expected in Mexico.

"It's all right, I imagine it must be something important. Do you care for coffee or something else?"

"Coffee will do ma'am."

Mrs. Velasco turned to the maid who had not left the room, ordered coffee for both of them and then invited Luis to be seated. After the maid came back, Mrs. Velasco poured out the coffee for Luis and then for her in an elegant set of white Noritake porcelain with navy-blue and gold rims, and dismissed the maid.

"Now Commander, what is it that you need to know?" inquired the lady.

"Ma'am, I am here because of the problem of Manolo Pardo. Have you heard about it?

"Yes, I heard from someone that he had been arrested in Houston trying to smuggle some drugs, although the newspapers did not have any story, that I know."

"That is correct, we believe that he has been framed."

"Just like General Humberto Mariles was?" she asked, with a touch of irony in her voice referring to the former Olympic equestrian champion, winner for Mexico of a gold medal at the London Olympics right after World War II. The general had been caught some years before trying to smuggle cocaine into Paris in a Mexican diplomatic pouch and claimed that he had been framed, just to later confess that he was in a very tight money situation and desperately needed cash.

"I believe Manolo was really framed, but in any case, that is what we are investigating, ma'am," answered Luis non-committaly.

"And how does that have anything to do with me?" her voice a little edgy.

"We believe that it might have been your daughter's father who had the cocaine placed in Manolo's bags," responded Luis.

Her beautiful face became paler as she exclaimed almost breathlessly, "Cesar?"

"Well ma'am I don't know his name," responded Luis.

"Cesar Velasco," she responded with a mechanical tone.

"Cesar Velasco. Is that your husband?" asked Luis noticing the last name.

"Yes."

"Ms. Velasco," said Luis, "I understand that your husband was a student at the University of Mexico who went to Cuba after the riots of 1968, studied there and became eventually a college professor who died long before Julieta was born in 1986, so he could not have been her father."

"Why are the Mexican police interested in this anyway?" She asked, disregarding Luis's comment, "It is a matter that concerns the Americans."

"The Mexican police are not interested in this," responded Luis.

Now it was her turn to be confused, "But, I thought..." she said, and the question trailed off.

"I said I was Commander Gil. I am a retired Federal Judicial Police Commander," explained Luis.

"Well sir, I feel you came into my house under false pretenses," she said, although her voice did not sound upset.

"Ma'am if I gave you the wrong impression, I apologize, I am a private investigator working for Manolo's grandfather, I just have this custom of using my rank out of habit."

"It's all right," she said, "You mentioned that Cesar could not have been Julieta's father."

"Please forgive me for any comments that might seem offensive ma'am, but I had assumed that Julieta's father had to be a man with whom you had a relationship after your marriage, and that he was obsessed by Julieta's death and was trying to get revenge."

Again she seemed to become paler and said, "The first part you got totally wrong, the second part may be true, I don't know."

"Ms. Velasco, would you care to explain?"

"I met Cesar Velasco in Cuba in 1976, I was only sixteen and I fell in love with him. Fidel Castro had all of us believing that we had to be thankful for the young men from all over Latin America that were coming to our universities to get an education and go back to their countries and help them shed the chains of colonial slavery. Beautiful words, the truth was that we were training terrorists to go back to their countries and subvert their governments."

"I suppose that when you are sixteen you are bound to believe anything," said Luis.

She smiled sadly while nodding and continued, "So, when I met Cesar, he was a hero to me. A dedicated political sciences professor and a confirmed revolutionary burning with desire to overthrow the Mexican government and install the dictatorship of proletariat. We married three months later in a 'revolutionary ceremony' as they called them, one hundred-plus couples getting married at the same time."

"I understand," said Luis.

"In 1978 we came to live in Mexico. Cesar disappeared in 1979. Just like that, one day we said good-bye, he was going to his work as a professor in the University, that night he did not return. I never saw Cesar Velasco again in my life."

"His parents, what happened to them?" asked Luis.

"I lived with them until his mother died, she never saw Cesar again either. His father is the senior partner in my accounting firm. He remarried, but I still consider him as my father, we are very close. He has never seen Cesar again either. I guess Cesar decided to leave and turn into a real revolutionary, that was his dream."

"So, what happened to him, do you know?" asked Luis.

"Yes, I do," she said, "Cesar Velasco was killed by the government while he tried to create a revolution in Mexico," she replied sadly.

"I am sorry, ma'am."

"Yes, I am very sorry too," she replied.

Luis was intrigued by the death of the lady's husband, but was more concerned about finding the truth on Julieta's father. "Now, it is obvious that if Cesar died in 1979, he could not have been Julieta's father," continued Luis.

"That is a long story," she said.

"I have all the time in the world," replied Luis getting hold of the thermos bottle that contained the coffee and offering her some, which she accepted by holding her cup so that Luis could pour some for her and then some for him.

"Very well," she started, "This is what happened."

After Ms. Velasco finished, Luis was stunned. This had to be the strangest story he had ever heard. Yet, everything made perfect sense.

After a long silence, he said: "Let me try to summarize what you have just told me. In essence, you are saying that Cesar Velasco was listed as killed by the Mexican Army after a failed uprising in the State of Chiapas in the year of 1979?"

"Right," she replied.

"A few years later, after his mother's death, Cesar reappeared in your life under a different name and you again lived with him for a few months, which was when you got pregnant of Julieta."

"Right."

"And that you left Cesar for good after you discovered that he had become a drug-trafficker.

"Uh-mhu."

Luis remained silent for a few seconds, then he said, "Well Ms. Velasco, I have taken enough of your time already, it's late and you must be tired, but I may have to talk to you again, you understand?"

"Call me anytime, I am as interested as you are in knowing what really happened. Julieta's death caused me a great pain and I guess I blamed Manolo for it."

"I understand," said Luis.

"In retrospect, nobody can blame another for the suicide of a child. I may be more to blame for not spending more time with her and for not inspiring on her more confidence to speak freely to me after she became pregnant." Those last words were said with such a tone of pain that Luis felt his stomach turn as he ached to take her in his arms and comfort her.

19

IMMINENT TRIAL

A couple of days later Roberto was going all over the Pardo file checking on the evidence to be used at trial when Dana called on the intercom advising that that Luis Gil was on the phone. Roberto answered, after a warm hello, Luis told him cryptically that he had some very important information on the case but needed to talk in person with him.

"Information from Ms. Velasco?" had asked Roberto.

"No," replied Luis, "Ms. Velasco did not want to help at all. I believe that she is the mistress of some top guy in the government and is afraid of telling. I spent almost three hours at her house just asking her questions and she just would not talk." When Roberto pressed him about who had given him the important information, Luis just said, "Our mutual friend from Monterrey."

There had never been any mention about someone from Monterrey, the large industrial city in northern Mexico, so Roberto understood that Luis did not want to talk on the phone.

_____

The following day Roberto had promised Dana, his secretary,

that he would take care of all the paperwork. It is amazing how much work it is to run a medium size law office. Mail and memos seem to pile up in an instant. Roberto did not like much doing office work, but it was necessary, particularly because the Pardo trial was now imminent and would require Roberto's full attention for the best part of two weeks.

He had spent all morning dispatching work and dictating letters and was already bored. He looked at his watch to see if it was true that it was only eleven, he was dying for it to be twelve so he would have the excuse of lunch. But no, it was still ten past eleven. 'Logical,' –he thought– 'five minutes ago it was five past eleven.'

The intercom buzzed. 'Good,' –thought Roberto– 'a telephone call.' Anything was better than processing paperwork.

Dana announced, "Roberto? Commander Gil on line four."

"Oh great!" answered Roberto, picking up the receiver, while Dana hung the phone on her end with a knowing smile on her face.

"Hello?"

"Hello my illustrious and learned attorney, how are you?" Luis seemed to be in a festive mood.

"Bored, but I can see you are not."

"Of course not. I have been sitting on a luxurious suede-covered sofa with a cup of excellent Colombian coffee in my left hand for the last hour-and-a-half without nothing to do but enjoy myself."

"Marvelous. Now that you have succeeded in completely ruining my day, answer me: when are we going to meet to discuss that information from our mutual Monterrey friend?"

"My dear friend that is exactly the point. I neglected to say that at this very precise moment I am looking out through the window of a Learjet flying at 50,000 feet en route to Houston."

"Is that right?" Roberto's enthusiasm was almost childish.

"Sure its right, this information is so important that Don Jose very nicely provided for my transportation so that we can talk face to face," replied Luis in his same playful mood.

"He should have sent the jet to pick me up so that we could speak in Mexico," said Roberto jokingly.

"My friend, you already had your fun coming twice in this case to visit this very nice country from where you voluntarily exiled yourself, now it's my turn to visit yours," answered Luis.

"Yeah, I guess you're right," said Roberto not very convinced, "Where do I pick you up, at Hobby?"

"That's the reason I'm calling. I had planned not to call you and then sneak into your office like a ghost and scare the living daylights out of you," said Luis while Roberto could not suppress a laugh, "But the pilots confronted me with this difficult question. Where should we land? I told them that counselor Duran would know the answer. You have all the answers. So, where do you want us to land?"

"I don't know... which airport is better?"

"Come on, you answer my question with a question, typical attorney. I now see that I will have to decide myself. Which one is closer to your office?"

"Oh... I guess... Intercontinental."

"That settles the matter. You see how easy things are when you leave important decisions in the hands of the police. You ambulance-chasers only complicate everything."

"It is all a matter of I.Q. my friend. We attorneys have such a high I.Q. that we have trouble approaching very simple problems. The primitive mind of a police officer is, on the other hand, ideal to resolve those same very simple problems."

After they both stopped laughing, they agreed to meet at the Business Aviation Terminal of Intercontinental in little over thirty minutes. The Learjet would be landing there before that time, but Roberto needed at least that much time to get to the airport.

Three hours later, they were both seated in the Las Alamedas restaurant on Katy Freeway. Roberto had picked up Luis at the airport and, after checking in Luis's room and leaving his bag at the Four Seasons Hotel, Luis and Roberto drove to Las Alamedas.

It was a Wednesday, so Roberto was not sure if they had their excellent buffet at the bar, but they could always sit in the restaurant and have lunch. It so happened that they did have the buffet, but it was going to start until three-thirty, so they sat at the bar and drank a couple of Stolichnaya tonics while they chatted.

Luis told Roberto everything about Ms. Velasco. Roberto did not speak until after Luis finished, when he asked, "Gee Luis, all this sounds like a fairy tale. Do you believe the whole story?"

"Yes I do," said Luis, "The lady was clearly telling the truth and if you think about it, it is pretty consistent with what Lupe told us."

"Yeah, right."

"Ms. Velasco also gave me a pretty good physical description of the man, and guess what Roberto?"

"What?"

"He matches a description of Julieta."

"What do you mean?" asked Roberto.

"Just that. He is very blond, green eyes, very tall for a Mexican, over 6-foot, with an athletic build."

"You're describing yourself Luis. Are you sure you are not the mysterious Cesar?" asked Roberto jokingly.

"You know, when she was giving me the description I felt like she was kind of describing me, other than I don't have very blond hair."

"Well you have light brown hair, and you can always dye it," joked Roberto and then asked "Have you asked Lupe Saldaña about Cesar?"

"Never on the phone, remember? Especially never mention

the name Cesar, he doesn't know that we know his name is Cesar, which is his real name. Every time I talk on the phone I say that Ms. Velasco did not want to cooperate. To say otherwise would be to endanger her. This man is really ruthless. Remember what I told you about the triggerman killing four guys because the boss thought one of them was cheating on him."

"You're right. We have to be very careful," said Roberto.

The waiter came to announce that the buffet was already served and they ordered two more Stolichnaya tonics and went to serve themselves some of the excellent food.

"This chicken mini-tacos and the guacamole are the best," said Roberto to Luis who was hesitating because of the abundance of delicious food.

After getting a generous dose of food, they went back to their table to continue talking.

"So, I guess you are going to visit Saldaña in person to ask him about our mysterious man?" said Roberto.

"Right, Don Jose instructed me to fly back into the hacienda of San Gabriel to talk with Lupe," replied Luis.

"Good," said Roberto, "The trial will be in three weeks. I need one week to prepare all the witnesses live, so we have a week left to investigate. To be honest, at this time, I really do not believe Lupe Saldaña will be able to find out anything more that is valuable for us."

"He may," responded Luis. "He told me he is working on a lead."

"Yes, but if he does not get anything pretty soon, Ms. Velasco may be what will carry the day. A jury will be hard-pressed to believe Manolo's allegations that he did not know that the cocaine was there. I need testimony from people without interest or even an interest adverse to that of Manolo. Do you think Ms. Velasco would be willing to tell that same story from the witness stand?"

"No Roberto, she is not going to testify."

"Have you asked her?"

"No, but she will not," said Luis with finality.

"Why don't you ask her, maybe she'll accept," insisted Roberto, with a conciliatory tone.

"No, I am not going to ask her, it would be too dangerous. This guy Cesar would kill her if he so much as suspects that she might testify," answered Luis.

"Oh... I seem to detect an interest that is more than mere professional, my friend," said Roberto with a teasing tone.

"You're crazy Roberto," said Luis with a slightly upset tone that demonstrated that Roberto was not crazy.

"Is the lady as pretty as the child?" asked Roberto remembering the picture that Manolo had asked his grandfather to send by messenger service to Roberto after their conversation. That picture showed a smiling, very beautiful young blond girl with pretty legs seated in a restaurant holding hands with Manolo.

"Prettier," responded Luis.

"That's it, you're hooked Luis. It's totally hopeless. You are in love with this woman," said Roberto with the same friendly teasing tone and a smile.

"Come on guy, you're out of your mind," answered Luis while his face blushed a little, "What happens is that you have chased one ambulance too many."

20

CRITICAL WITNESS

A phone ringing woke up Luis. As usual when you are suddenly awakened, for a split second he asked himself where he was. Then he realized that he was in Houston, in the Four Seasons Hotel. He straightened just enough on the bed to pick up the receiver.

"Hello?" he answered with a mushy voice.

"Commander Gil?" it was a woman's voice in Spanish and it sounded familiar to Luis, but at that instant he could not tell for sure who it was.

"Yes, who is this?" he said.

"Julieta Velasco," she answered.

Luis suddenly straightened up and put his legs down on the floor in a sitting position to the side of the bed, his mind could only think of the young girl who had committed suicide.

"Who?" He said incredulously.

"Julieta Velasco, Julieta's mother," she explained.

"Oh, I'm sorry Ms. Velasco, I am still half asleep."

"I am the one who is sorry to have called you at this time," she replied, "But it is important. Also, please don't call me Ms. Velasco, it makes me feel like a dinosaur."

"I'll be glad to call you Julieta, if you call me Luis instead of Commander Gil," said Luis.

"I will," she said, "Luis, I have something really important to tell you."

"Yes?"

"Cesar called me fifteen minutes ago."

"What?" Luis was totally awake now.

"Just what I said. He called and I was as surprised as you are now."

It was not until then that Luis realized that there was no way she could have known he was in Houston staying at the Four Seasons Hotel. The only one who could have told her was Terry, his secretary, but it was unlikely Terry would have given her the information without first getting authorization from Luis.

"How did you know I was here," he asked.

"Cesar told me, " she replied.

"Julieta, can you please explain," said Luis still feeling a little strange to call this beautiful woman by her first name.

"Cesar just called and woke me up to say that he knew I had met with you two days ago, that you had been asking about him and that I was the only one who could have told you about him," she said.

Luis felt his heart freeze at those words. It meant that she was in danger. The feeling surprised him, but he did not say anything while she continued.

"So, I told him that it was true. That I had told you about him and so what? He was not happy, of course, but there is nothing he can do," she concluded.

"How can you say that, don't you know your husband?" said Luis.

"Yes I do. I know he is not going to do anything bad to me," she said, with a sense of security that Luis was very far from sharing.

"But how did he know that you had told me about him and that I was in Houston."

"I have no idea, but he knew, and then he said that I better call you to tell you to stop asking questions if you do not want to get hurt."

Luis's mind raced, 'Did she sound worried?' –he thought–.

"So I told him I would have to wait until the morning, I don't have your home phone--"

"It's 5524-4752 and my cell phone is 044-5537-9292," interrupted Luis, who wanted to be sure that she had all his phone numbers.

"Thanks," she said, "Let me write them down. Hold it a second." There was a pause, while she looked for a pen and wrote the numbers, then she continued, "But Cesar said that I better call you right away. He said you were in Houston, at the Four Seasons Hotel. He even gave me your room number."

Luis had not turned on the light, there was some light filtering in through the curtains that semi-covered the large window, but after hearing those words he turned the light on, pulled out the Beretta, which was under his pillow, and looked all around. Julieta's words made him feel as if the walls had eyes that were looking at him.

Julieta continued, "Cesar said that you had been dining with an attorney from Houston by the name of Roberto Duran."

Luis felt shudders in his spine when he heard all that, he said, "What else did he tell you?" and his voice sounded hoarse even to his own ears.

"That Mr. Duran had suggested that I needed to testify at Manolo's trial and that you had refused," she continued, "Cesar said that you were right, that it would be very dangerous for both, you and me, if I testified."

"What else did he say?"

"Nothing more, that's all," she responded.

"Uhmm," said Luis because he did not know what to say, then he asked, "How come you are not afraid of him hurting you?"

"Oh, Cesar would never hurt me," she answered candidly but with absolute certainty in her voice.

For some reason, the comment made Luis feel terribly uncomfortable, but he only said, "I wish I could feel equally confident Julieta."

"You can be. Anyway, the reason I'm calling is to tell you that I will testify at the trial. What Cesar just said convinced me that he framed Manolo. I am not going to let Manolo go to jail to satisfy Cesar's desire for revenge."

There was a silence. After a moment, Luis said, "Yes, I figured that is what you were going to do. We have to be extremely careful. Cesar has eyes everywhere and is very powerful and ruthless. Please be very careful Julieta." His last words had a tone of concern.

She simply said, "I will, don't worry."

Next morning Roberto picked up Luis at the Four Seasons and on the way to Intercontinental Luis told him about the call of the night before. They both pondered trying to find an explanation and concluded that Cesar had to have kept them under surveillance and then, using probably a long-distance microphone, overheard their whole conversation at Las Alamedas. It seemed far-fetched but was the only logical explanation and Roberto knew, from the many trials in which he had worked in as a court interpreter that the technology was available.

Because Luis had no rush to get to the airport - the pilots had readied the Learjet to take off at any time convenient for Luis - Roberto decided to stop at Bobby Cavazos's office and asked him to make an electronic sweep of his BMW. Bobby did so and declared the car not tampered with and gave Roberto an infrared sensor to detect the use of any long-distance mike nearby. Bobby then promised that he would visit Roberto's office and house and check all the spaces and phone lines to try to prevent any eavesdropping.

Slightly less tense by Bobby's assurances, but still aware that counter-detection was not 100% safe, Roberto and Luis boarded the BMW, and on route to the airport decided that Luis would fly to Lupe and that both Lupe and Luis would try to piece the puzzle together by attempting to locate the man identified by the triggerman as the person who had actually carried out the changing of Manolo's bags at the airport. Also, Don Jose would be asked to provide security for Ms. Velasco now that she had told Luis that she was going to testify. Both Roberto and Luis were sure that Cesar already knew about that conversation. It was a lot easier to place a bug in a private residence or in a hotel room than to eavesdrop a conversation at a restaurant.

As usual when important cases are nearing trial, two weeks flew by with activities going into a crescendo. Ms. Velasco had been placed under protective custody by the security services of Bancomer in Don Jose's house at Las Brisas. Lupe continued trying to find out the location of the man pointed out by the triggerman, but the man seemed to have vanished without a trace.

At the final pre trial conference, set for a Friday one week before the date for trial, Roberto re-urged his motion to suppress the cocaine found in Manolo's bags based on the fact that the agent who testified at the detention hearing had stated that no tip had been received. The Judge heard only a proffer by both Roberto and Bill Block, the Assistant U.S. Attorney in charge of the case, and denied the motion, as Roberto fully expected. Customs officers have an almost absolute discretion for inspections at the border or its functional equivalent, such as airports, when the traveler is making first entry into the country.

Roberto had also moved for disclosure of the identity of the tipster and the Judge ordered the government to provide the identity and any criminal record the tipster had. The informant's identity proved to be a useless piece of information. She had been working with Continental as a gate agent but had disappeared almost contemporaneously with the tip. It was obvious that Cesar had transferred her to some other part of his organization after giving the tip.

The last motion filed by Roberto was for disclosure of the files of all law enforcement agents who had participated in Manolo's arrest. Roberto knew most of the officers had impeccable records, but Roberto also knew that Michael Carroll, the member of the anti-drug task force who had actually handcuffed Manolo, had a pretty bad record of brutality. Block argued strenuously against disclosure but the Judge granted the motion. The government had three days to disclose to the defense the personnel records of the arresting officers.

Finally, the Judge set the trial to go at 9 a.m. on Monday, a week from the following Monday. The trial would start in one week.

———————————————————

It was to be hectic week. All the participants were already in Houston on Monday, a week before the trial. Roberto wanted them to be available to drill them intensively on the direct and cross-examinations they would have to undergo. Ms. Velasco, as the most critical witness, was to be the person with whom Roberto, Luis, Bobby Cavazos and two of Roberto's associate attorneys would spend the longest time. Roberto hoped that Ms. Velasco's testimony would sway the jury to believe that Manolo's story was true. The problem was that the testimony was for the most part hearsay and basically unrelated to the main facts, but it was which certainly explained and made those facts credible.

Roberto also had to work on all possible scenarios for the

cross-examination of the government witnesses, mainly for the testimony that Roberto strongly suspected Michael Carroll, the officer that had arrested Manolo, was going to give. The week would go by in a sigh.

Friday, with tension ringing in the air, Roberto sent all the witnesses away with a last admonition to relax and rest during the weekend. He suspected that it would be the last chance they all would have to relax for at least a week.

21

THE TRIAL BEGINS

On the fateful Monday, at 9:10 the Judge came into the courtroom and called the case. The government, by and through Bill Block, Assistant U.S. Attorney, announced ready. Roberto announced ready for the defense.

"Are there any matters that we need to take up before selecting the jury," asked the Judge.

"Not for the government, Your Honor," said Block.

"Neither for the defense, Your Honor," said Roberto.

"Very well, call the panel in," said the Judge.

The jury panelists were summoned in and the process of jury selection began. It was a boring process but Roberto knew how extremely important it was, so all his senses concentrated on it.

The name of jury selection is really a misnomer, what actually takes place is that both the government and the defense try to eliminate those jurors they perceive to be biased by executing their peremptory and for cause strikes. Of those panelists not stricken, the first 14 names are called.

In Federal Court the process is relatively short because, as opposed to State Courts, the attorneys do not question the panel directly but through the Judge. Shortly before 12:00, a jury had been selected. The Judge, looking at his watch, sent everybody to an early lunch after advising them to be back at exactly 1:00 p.m. to start the trial.

Back into the courtroom, Roberto felt his stomach tightening. A criminal trial is a chess game where the stakes are the freedom of a human being.

"Before we start, Your Honor, the Government would like to invoke the rule," said Bill Block.

Invoking the rule means that the witnesses would have to wait outside the courtroom until called to testify so that they will not be able to hear what the others are testifying, but testify only as to what they personally remembered. Roberto had planned to invoke it but Block had taken the initiative.

There are several exceptions to the rule and Roberto, relying on one of them, asked the Judge to allow Luis Gil and Bobby Cavazos, who were both in Roberto's witness list, although he did not believe they would be testifying, to stay in the courtroom as his investigators and sit at the defense table. The Judge allowed it. Also, Don Jose, his wife Doña Rosita, and Bertha, Manolo's mother, who were not to be called to testify could remain in the courtroom in the spectators' section and, of course, the defendant has to be present inside the courtroom to confront his accusers.

Before ordering the jury to be brought to the courtroom, the Judge asked Roberto, "Will you be needing an interpreter at all Mr. Duran? Even without you, our interpreters are still very good," he said with a smile. Roberto had been the Chief Interpreter of the Federal Court for several years.

Roberto smiled also and standing up, replied, "No, Your Honor, my client is very fluent in English and all my witnesses are able to testify in English."

"Very well then, bring in the jury," ordered the judge to his case manager.

As soon as all the 12 jurors plus 2 alternates were seated, the Judge gave his opening remarks to the jury. As usual, he explained that, first the government would make its initial argument and that the defense could, but did not have to, make an initial argument as well. The defense could reserve the right to make an initial argument at a later time, at the beginning of the defense case. Initial arguments are simply an outline of what the parties expect the evidence to show. Then the government would call its witnesses one by one, whom the defense could cross-examine. The defense could, but did not have to call witnesses and the process would be reversed, with the defense attorney asking the direct questions and the government cross-examining the defense witnesses.

Finally, the parties would make their respective final arguments. The government had the right to open and close the final arguments because the government had, as in all criminal cases, the burden of proving the defendant guilty beyond all reasonable doubt. The Judge reminded the jury that the defendant has the absolute right to remain silent and that no inference could be made out of the desire of the defendant not to testify, and, of course, that the defendant begins the trial with a completely clean slate. Because of the presumption of innocence, it is the government's burden to prove a defendant guilty and if the government fails to do so, the jury must acquit the defendant.

After the Judge finished, Block stood up. Roberto normally always made an initial argument to sense how the jury responded, but in this particular case he had already decided to reserve his initial argument for until after the government rested. It was simply a matter of tactics, he wanted the government to put on their case before evaluating how the jury responded to his own argument.

Block was famous for his initial arguments. Not because they were very good, but because they were very lengthy and pretty boring, which suited Roberto just fine. True to his reputation, Block explained in unnecessary detail the very simple facts of how the cocaine had been discovered and Manolo arrested. The obvious implication of the argument being that Manolo was a high-flying drug trafficker who had decided this time to make a delivery in person instead of using his mules.

Roberto was delighted. For one thing, it would be relatively easy to destroy the theory of Manolo being a drug lord, a few strategic questions would do the job, and Roberto could see that the jurors were getting bored. By the end of Block's presentation, Roberto even detected a few drowsy pairs of eyes.

After Block finished, the Judge asked Roberto if he was going to make an opening argument.

"I will, Your Honor, but I reserve it for the beginning of our case," replied Roberto.

"Very well. Mr. Block, call your first witness," said the Judge.

Block called as his first witness the agent who had testified at the detention hearing before the magistrate. Roberto had assumed that he was going to do so because he wanted to do some damage control by bringing out into the open right at the beginning of the trial the fact that the man had perjured himself. Block would try to cure the agent's perjury. If he did not succeed, it would be easier that the jury might forget about the perjury right now than if called at a later time and, in any case, it would give the impression of being very straightforward.

The direct examination proceeded uneventfully. The only change to his earlier story was that this time the agent did acknowledge that there had been an informant tipping the Customs Service about Manolo.

That was when Block asked, "Agent, at the detention hearing you testified that you had been called to the site of the Customs examination after the cocaine was discovered, right?"

The witness then spurted out, "Yes sir, that is what I said, but I was wrong, because actually I--"

"Allow me to interrupt you, Agent," said Block, a little flustered. "You did testify what I just said at the detention hearing, right?"

"Yes, sir."

"But you were wrong about it, you were not called after the Customs inspector found the cocaine, in fact, you had been standing next to the defendant from the moment he was referred to that inspector, is that right?" asked Block.

"Objection, leading," said Roberto standing up.

"Try not to lead, Mr. Block," said the Judge.

The agent looked to the Judge not knowing what to do and the Judge said, "Go ahead, you can answer."

"That is right, yes sir," responded the agent.

"Why did you answer to defense counsel that you had not been standing there, but rather had been called later?" continued Block, trying to purge the agent's prior testimony.

"Because I did not understand the question," responded the witness.

Roberto could not help but smile. The agent had obviously selected a very feeble excuse to try and cure his perjury.

"That is all I have, Your Honor. Pass the witness," responded Block.

"I just have a few questions. Agent, at the detention hearing you testified that there were no agents standing next to Mr. Pardo while his bags were being inspected, right?" asked Roberto.

"Right, because I did not understand your question, sir," answered the agent.

"At that time I asked you if it was customary to have five agents waiting while the luggage of an individual is being inspected, do you remember?" said Roberto.

"Eh... yes," responded the agent.

"You answered that you did not understand my question, right?" asked Roberto.

"I believe I did, yes," said the agent.

"Then, that was the question you did not understand?" continued Roberto, with a very friendly tone, hoping that the man had not read a transcript of the hearing and would bite his hook.

"Exactly. I did not understand the question," answered the agent, now a little less nervous at the reassuring tone of Roberto.

"But you did understand all the other questions asked?" said Roberto, with the same friendly tone.

"Eh... yes, I guess I did," answered the agent, now less sure of where the questioning was going.

"So why did you answer that you had not been standing next to Mr. Pardo?" asked Roberto, his tone becoming threatening.

"Eh... ah... sir, ah... I... it was just that, ah... I did not understand the question," answered the agent.

"I thought you just said that you had understood all the other questions?" asked Roberto.

"Objection, Your Honor, the agent said 'I guess I did', not I did," said Block standing up.

"Overruled," said the Judge. "Answer please," to the witness.

"I'm sorry, I believe I did not understand the question of the attorney," said the agent, addressing the Judge.

"Do you understand this? Were you standing next to Mr. Pardo at the time he was being inspected?" asked the Judge with exasperation.

"Yes," said the agent.

"Yes, you understand, or yes, you were standing next to Mr. Pardo?" continued the Judge, slightly raising his voice.

"Yes, I was standing next to Mr. Pardo when he was being inspected," replied the agent.

"Go ahead Mr. Duran," said the Judge.

Roberto, reading from the transcript of the detention hearing, asked, "Agent, at the detention hearing, the Magistrate Judge, after overruling an objection from the prosecutor, asked, and I quote, 'Were there any agents standing next to the defendant at the time of his inspection, yes or no?' and you responded, 'No ma'am, there were not.' When were you telling the truth? At the time you answered to the Magistrate Judge what I just read, or right now when you answered the question of His Honor?"

The agent looked toward the prosecutor trying to get some support, but Block looked away from him. Roberto was looking, not at the witness, but at the jury. He liked what he saw. The jurors were all looking intently at the agent, waiting for his answer.

"Eh... eh... ah... I just did not understand it, that is all," said the agent, now paler than a white sheet of paper.

"No more questions, pass the witness, Your Honor," said Roberto with a disgusted tone, while discreetly looking at the jury. It was clear they had not liked what the agent had said.

With the opening argument of Block and the afternoon recess taken after Block finished, it was now almost 4 o'clock and the Judge had announced that they would adjourn early because he had some other matters he had to take, so the Judge then called for the overnight recess. Everybody in the courtroom stood up for the jury to leave the room. After the jury left, before getting up to leave, the Judge asked Block to give him an idea of his schedule. Block replied that he was hoping to call three more witnesses for the following day, "I believe the government can be resting tomorrow afternoon, Your Honor," ended Block.

"What about your case, Mr. Duran?" asked the Judge.

"I have five or six witnesses, Your Honor, at least two are factual witnesses and will take the best part of two days. The others are character witnesses and should not take long." said Roberto.

"Good, I will see you tomorrow," said the Judge.

22

PERJURY

T uesday morning the Judge asked if there was something they needed to do out of the presence of the jury. Block stood up and said, "Your Honor, the government had three more witnesses. Officers Fields and Carroll and a chemist from the D.E.A. Central Lab in Dallas, but Officer Fields has been sent on an emergency mission out of Houston, so I only have two more witnesses."

Roberto became tense. Fields and Carroll, together with the rookie, had jumped on Manolo and roughed him quite a bit. Roberto was relying on Fields to tell the story about why they jumped on Manolo. With Fields gone, Roberto felt possible that Carroll might make something up to justify the roughness, so he stood up and objected strenuously to no avail.

The Judge said, "Mr. Duran, as you well know, the government is free to call any witnesses they have announced previously, or to refuse to call them. Besides, you can always subpoena officer Fields if you feel you need his testimony. Very well, bring in the jury and Mr. Block, call your next witness."

"The government calls Mr. Anderson, the chemist," said Block.

The testimony of the chemist was as boring as can be expected. Everybody in the courtroom was falling asleep. In almost every case Roberto would stipulate that the substance found was in fact cocaine to avoid the waste of time of holding the government to prove it, but this was a case where Roberto would never dispense with the cross-examination of the chemist, it was one of the strong points of his case.

After Block passed the witness, Roberto asked, "Mr. Anderson, the cocaine found in my client's luggage was contained in clear plastic bags, is that right?"

"Yes sir, that's right."

"Did you perform any fingerprint tests to determine if the fingerprints of Mr. Pardo, my client, could be found on any of the plastic bags?" The lab never carries out such tests because it is almost impossible to get good latent prints from the bags.

"No Mr. Duran, we did not," answered the chemist.

"But you have the capabilities to perform those tests, did you not?" countered Roberto.

"Yes sir, we do," answered the chemist and then went on to explain that most of the times it is worthless to perform them.

"But there was still a possibility that good latent fingerprints could have been obtained from the bags, is that right?" asked Roberto.

"Everything is possible, that is right, yes."

"And then the government could have said with absolute certainty that my client knew about the cocaine because he obviously had touched it, right?" said Roberto.

"Objection, Your Honor, calls for speculation," jumped Block.

"Withdrawn," said Roberto before the Judge made a ruling on Block's objection. "Mr. Anderson, among the many and very detailed questions of the prosecution..." asked Roberto with a slightly ironic tone, "I do not remember that the purity of the cocaine was ever asked. Can you tell me what degree of purity was the cocaine found in my client's bags?"

"It was 30%, sir," answered the chemist.

"Thirty percent!" asked Roberto, as if extremely surprised.

"Yes sir."

"Is that common, Mr. Anderson? Is most of the cocaine seized at a port of entry which you test 30%?" asked Roberto, again with a tone of surprise, although he knew the answer perfectly well.

"No, it is very uncommon, sir, most of the cocaine seized at ports of entry varies between 90% and 98%," said the chemist.

"That is, of course, because the cocaine is then cut down with diluting agents to make more of it, right?" asked Roberto.

"Yes sir."

"Because it would be an absurdity to bring cocaine at 30% when you could bring it at 95% and then cut it down and make 4 or 5 times as much to sell on the street, right?" asked Roberto.

"Right," answered the chemist succinctly.

"Have you ever seen drugs confiscated in a port of entry with such purity?" Roberto decided to stretch his luck.

"Not really, sir. The cocaine that has purity around 30% is normally the cocaine that is caught on the streets, after it has been cut down," answered the chemist.

"Thank you, Mr. Anderson, I pass the witness, Your Honor."

The Judge looked at his watch, the lengthy direct examination had taken so much that it was time for the lunch break and so they made a one-hour recess.

After lunch, the Judge said, "Go ahead, Mr. Block, call your next witness."

"The government calls Agent Carroll, Your Honor," replied Block.

Roberto's stomach tightened at the mention of the name. This was the witness he was really concerned about.

Block started with the usual questions to introduce the witness and made Carroll give a detailed narrative of the events on the day Manolo was arrested.

"So, what did you personally do after you saw the white

powdery substance that subsequent lab analysis has demonstrated was cocaine?" was asking Block in his peculiar convoluted style.

"I ordered the suspect to lie down on the floor," answered Carroll and Roberto could not repress a smile at the euphemism in the answer.

"After you had the suspect lying on the floor, what next did you do to secure the suspect as required by proper law enforcement procedures?" continued Block.

"I handcuffed him from the back, then ordered him to stand up and read him his Miranda rights," answered Carroll. "It was then that I noticed that the suspect had wet his pants."

Block disregarded the last answer and the direct examination continued in great detail until it was established that Manolo had been taken into an interrogation room in the airport and held incommunicado for several hours. Roberto knew that Carroll had been in the room by himself with Manolo at certain points in time, which was what worried him the most.

Block was then asking, "It came a point in which Officer Fields left the room and you were left with the defendant alone. Could you tell the jury what transpired then?"

"After Charlie walked out, the suspect turned to me and said, 'Okay, you caught me red handed, is there any way we could work this out--'"

"¡Hijo de la chingada, está mintiendo, Roberto!" said Manolo trying to whisper, but his anger made him speak loud enough for everybody in the courtroom to hear it.

The Judge turned to look sternly at the defense table and was about to say something when he saw Roberto with a finger across his lips while Luis Gil was holding Manolo from the shoulder. The Judge then just turned to the witness and said, "Go ahead, continue."

Carroll, who understood enough Spanish to know that Manolo had said, "Son of a bitch, he is lying, Roberto," had a thin smile on his lips when he continued, "That is all he said, so I told him that there was a good way to work it out if he wanted to cooperate with the government and give us all the names of his associates in the criminal conspiracy."

"What did he answer to that?" asked Block.

"Just then Fields returned and the suspect closed like a clam, said that he did not want to speak anymore with us and asked for an attorney, so immediately we suspended any questioning and took him to the detention center," answered Carroll.

"Did you have any more involvement in the case after that, Officer Carroll?" continued Block.

"No sir, that was it."

"You did assist in preparing the report, did you not?" asked Block.

"Yes sir."

"In the report there is no mention of what you just testified, why is that?" asked Block. It was a way to preempt Roberto's cross-examination, which would obviously concentrate on the fact that the report mentioned no admission by Manolo.

"I did not consider it important enough, suspects very often make strange comments and we cannot include every one in the reports," answered Carroll.

"I understand," replied Block and then continued, "As a matter of fact, you did not consider it important enough to even mention it to me until this very morning, is that correct?"

"That is correct sir, I only mentioned it to you this morning, downstairs, in the prosecutor's office in this building," replied Carroll imperturbably.

"Thank you very much, Officer Carroll. Pass the witness, Your Honor," said Block standing up.

"You may proceed Mr. Duran," said the Judge.

"Thank you, Your Honor. Officer Carroll, how long have you been a law enforcement officer?"

"Over eighteen years," answered Carroll, who had seemed to

lose some of his good humor. He had good reason, he had been subjected to Roberto's cross-examination before and knew what to expect.

"And in those eighteen years you have not learned that an admission by a suspect is one of the most important bits of information for the prosecution?"

"What I've learned is that many times what we officers out there on the streets consider important is not important at all to you attorneys," answered Carroll, who had noticed that the prosecutor had clearly disassociated himself from the testimony he was now giving by pointing out that Carroll had not mentioned anything earlier.

"Very true," said Roberto with fake patience, "And that is exactly why you, as law enforcement officers, are supposed to tell everything to the prosecutor so that he or she, being an attorney, will be able to evaluate a case?"

"Argumentative, Your Honor," jumped Block.

"It's cross-examination, Judge," countered Roberto.

"I'll allow it," said the Judge.

"Well, I did not think the prosecutor would be interested," answered Carroll, sticking to his story.

"Yeah, but what about your supervisor or your fellow officers, they would not have been interested either?" asked Roberto heatedly.

"Is it a question, or are you testifying, counselor," replied Carroll, now becoming openly aggressive.

"Your Honor, could you instruct the witness to answer the question," said Roberto.

"Mr. Carroll," said the Judge in a stern voice, "As I am sure you know with all your years in law enforcement, in a courtroom, witnesses are expected to answer questions, not ask them."

"I'm sorry, Sir," said Carroll, who did not show any contrition.

"Go ahead, Mr. Duran," said the Judge to Roberto.

"What has me a little bit confused, Mr. Carroll, is that you testified that my client, 'Closed like a clam,' I believe those were your exact words, after you told him that in order to work out things he had to give you names of co-conspirators. Did I understand that correctly?"

"Yes, you did," answered Carroll.

"It was then that Officer Fields came back to the room and my client asked for an attorney, right?" asked Roberto.

"Right," answered Carroll.

"Yet, one of the reports states that Officer Fields came back to the room for the last time about twenty minutes before my client requested an attorney?"

"That is correct, yes. What happened is that when I said before, 'Right then Charlie returned,' what I meant was simply that, after Charlie came back into the room, the suspect would not answer any more questions," said Carroll.

"When you say Charlie, you refer to Officer Fields?" asked Roberto.

"Fields, yes. Charles Fields," replied Carroll.

"But your report says, let me read it," said Roberto turning over to get the piece of paper that Bobby Cavazos was handing him where Bobby had highlighted the relevant portion, "'Officers Fields and Carroll then continued the interrogation together for about twenty minutes after Officer Fields came back into the room. After that, the suspect requested an attorney and interrogation was immediately discontinued.' That is what your report says. May I approach the witness Your Honor," finished Roberto, turning to the Judge.

"Go ahead," said the Judge.

"This is your report, and that is what it says, if you want to look at it," said Roberto.

"Your Honor, I object that the witness is testifying from a document that is not in evidence," said Block.

"I was about to offer it into evidence," countered Roberto.

"I still object that the document is highlighted, Your Honor," objected Block again.

"We will provide an unmarked copy for the jury, Your Honor, and I will offer it into evidence," said Roberto.

"Go ahead, set your foundation," replied the Judge.

"Officer, I hand you what has been marked for identification purposes only as defendant's exhibit 1, do you recognize it?" said Roberto, giving Carroll the copy.

"Yes, it's my report of the incident," said Carroll.

"The prosecutor has obviously examined it, he gave me the copy that I have. I offer it as defendant's exhibit 1."

"Objections?" asked the Judge, turning to Block. When Block shook his head, the judge ruled, "It's admitted."

"Now, Officer Carroll, what I read before is what your report says, am I correct?" asked Roberto.

"Yes, that is what it says," replied Carroll.

"But before, you had said that as soon as Fields returned my client closed like a clam. That is not what the report states."

"Everything is relative counselor," said Carroll with a cynical smile on his face.

"What do you mean by that?"

"Well, that when I said that, 'Right then Charlie returned and the suspect refused to answer,' I meant simply that he did not say anything incriminating any more," answered Carroll.

"How very convenient," said Roberto.

"Objection to the sidebar, Your Honor," jumped Block.

"I'm sorry, I was muttering to myself," said Roberto to the Judge.

The Judge could not suppress a smile but said, "No sidebar remarks Mr. Duran, please."

"Now, going back to the moment of the arrest," asked Roberto going back to his chair at the defense table, "You said that you ordered the suspect to lie on the floor?"

"That's right."

"Isn't it true that you actually jerked him down to the ground by forcibly grabbing him from the neck and hair and throwing him down?" asked Roberto.

"When you are making an arrest of a drug suspect counselor you don't use silk gloves," replied Carroll with his same cynical tone and attitude.

"So then you admit that you lied when you said before that you ordered him to lie down?" continued Roberto.

"I did not lie, I ordered him, and at the same time forced him down," replied Carroll without even a blink.

"Oh, I see. And of course you also lied when you said that you ordered him to get up after handcuffing him?" asked Roberto.

"I just ordered him to get up, that's all," said Carroll.

"Why then did you tear my client's silk jacket at the time you jerked him up?" asked Roberto.

"Silk is very delicate counselor," replied Carroll, with an ironical tone.

Roberto smiled, partly because of the comment, but mainly because Manolo's jacket had not been torn, it was just a trick by Roberto, who was not under oath to tell the truth, as the jury had already been told.

"You also said," he continued, "That my client had wet his pants, did you mean that he went to the bathroom in his trousers?"

"He urinated in his underwear, if you want it clearer counselor," said Carroll.

"Thank you Officer Carroll, that was clear enough," said Roberto seeing with the corner of his eye that Manolo had blushed openly, "Have you seen many hardened criminals urinate their underwear, Officer Carroll."

"A few, specially the bosses," replied Carroll.

Roberto was hoping Carroll would answer precisely in that way. It was needed for his next question. "That is because bosses never expect to be caught, right?"

"I guess so," replied Carroll, wondering where the questions were headed.

"And that is because bosses never get even slightly close to the drugs, isn't that right?" continued Roberto.

"Not necessarily, sometimes they may decide that they do not have anybody to trust and make a delivery themselves," said Carroll.

"Do you mean to say that a boss would risk his skin to deliver only sixty pounds?" asked Roberto with a mocking tone, but praying inwardly that Carroll would bite the hook.

"Sixty pounds after being cut down make up to 250 or 300 hundred pounds at street level, that means millions of dollars counselor," answered Carroll, turning cynical again.

"Oh yes, because you dilute the substance four or five times before selling it, right?" said Roberto, with a pensive but friendly tone.

"That's right," replied Carroll, a little surprised that Roberto sounded so friendly.

"So in your opinion, no boss in his right mind would risk his skin transporting cocaine that is already diluted?" asked Roberto.

"Objection, calls for speculation," jumped Block, almost yelling.

"Sustained," said the Judge.

It was speculation and the Judge had sustained the objection but Roberto, who had counted on the fact that dishonest police officers are also extremely sloppy and was sure Carroll had not read the chemist's report, just wanted to point it out for the jury.

The last thing Roberto wanted to impress on the jury was the subject of his next question, "Why were you kicked out of the Houston Police Department, Mr. Carroll?"

"Objection, Your Honor, assumes facts not in evidence," said Block.

"The Officer can tell Mr. Duran if his question is wrong, Mr.

Block. Go ahead and answer Officer Carroll," said the Judge now addressing the witness.

"I was not kicked out, I resigned," answered Carroll, but his face was a little blushed now.

"Why did you *resign*?" asked Roberto emphasizing the word 'resign.'

"Wanted better pay, the D.E.A. gave it to me," answered Carroll, regaining his composure.

But his composure did not last long. Roberto then stated, more than asked, "Isn't it true that you were forced to resign because Internal Affairs was investigating the twentieth or so complaint against you for police brutality?"

"Counselor, police work is hard work. If wimps do not like the way we do it, too bad," his face was red and his attitude extremely belligerent.

"Pass the witness Your Honor, I do not have any more questions."

"Any redirect Mr. Block," asked the Judge.

Block hesitated a little, but just stood up and said, "Nothing Your Honor."

"Very well, call your next witness," said the Judge while most of the jurors looked at their watches and, noticing it was almost 6:30, moved restlessly on their chairs. The Judge knew that there were no more witnesses.

Standing up Block said, "The government rests, Your Honor."

"Ladies and gentlemen, the government has rested, which means that they have presented all the evidence they planned to present in their case in chief. Please remember all my instructions and I will see you tomorrow to start promptly at 9:00 in the morning."

Once the jurors were out, the Judge turned to Roberto and asked, "Do you have any motions Mr. Duran."

"Yes Your Honor, at this time Mr. Manuel Pardo, by and through his attorney of record, moves for a judgment of acquittal on the grounds that the government has presented no evidence to prove guilt beyond a reasonable doubt, or in the alternative, that the evidence is insufficient therefor," replied Roberto. It was just a technical exercise necessary to preserve certain rights for appeal. Roberto was certain that the Court would not grant such a motion in this case.

"Mr. Block?" asked the Judge turning to the prosecutor.

"You have heard the evidence Your Honor, it is more than sufficient for the jury to find that Mr. Pardo did in fact possess with intent to distribute the cocaine," Block simply articulated the legal standard.

"Judgment of acquittal is denied. Gentlemen, I will see you tomorrow at nine for the defense case," said the Judge.

23

CESAR'S REVENGE

Wednesday morning, after the jury was brought into the courtroom, the Judge turned to Block and said, "You announced yesterday that you were resting Mr. Block."

"That is correct, Your Honor," responded Block after standing up.

"Ladies and gentlemen of the jury, it will now be the turn of the defendant to present any evidence he wishes, but always remember that a defendant does not have any obligation to present evidence."

Then the Judge turned to Roberto and said: "Very well, Mr. Duran, you reserved your opening argument. Will you make an opening argument now?"

"Yes Your Honor, thank you."

Roberto, who had stood up, walked toward the jury box, paused for a short moment and looked intently at the jury members while he began to speak. "Ladies and gentlemen of the jury, as the Judge told you at the beginning of this case, you are here to decide the guilt or innocence of the defendant, Mr. Manuel Pardo. It is an awesome responsibility. Yet this awesome responsibility will be discharged in this particular case by answering a very simple question: Did Mr. Pardo know that there was cocaine secreted in the bags that he presented to Customs, or did he not know it?"

Roberto always felt that the best tactics is to simplify the facts to the most. He continued, "The Judge told you that it is the obligation of the government to prove the case beyond a reasonable doubt, that the defendant does not need to present any evidence to prove his innocence. Yet, in this case I believe it can be said that the defendant will in fact prove his innocence."

"The Judge also told you that the defendant has the right to remain silent and that you may never conclude that he is guilty because he does not testify. Yet, in this case Mr. Pardo will in fact testify and will tell you, that he did not know that those *particular* bags contained cocaine."

Roberto paused again while he surveyed the reactions of the jurors with keen eyes. He liked what he saw. "I said those *particular* bags because as it will be brought to light in the defense case, what really happened in this case was that Mr. Pardo was the victim of a powerful drug lord who set a trap for him to be caught with cocaine in his bags and be sent to prison to get revenge for something that happened between the defendant, Mr. Pardo, and this mysterious man, whom you will find out is called Cesar."

Several members of the jury turned to look at Manolo, as Roberto expected them to do. There was curiosity in those eyes. "So, you see, this awesome responsibility will be very easy to fulfill. Just listen to the defense case and at the end you will be almost forced to reach the only verdict possible in this case, that of not guilty. Thank you."

"Go ahead Mr. Duran, call your first witness," said the Judge after Roberto had gone back to his table.

"The defense calls Mrs. Julieta Velasco, Your Honor."

"Call her name," ordered the Judge.

Julieta came into the courtroom. She was dressed soberly but very elegantly.

After she took the oath and sat at the witness stand, Roberto asked: "Ma'am, would you give us your full name for the record please?"

"Julieta Velasco,"

"You are not in any way related to the defendant, are you?"

"No sir. I know him but there is no family relationship," she answered.

"Mrs. Velasco, where were you born?"

"In Havana, Cuba."

"But you are now a Mexican citizen, is that correct?"

"Yes sir, I am," she said.

"That is because you married a Mexican, right?"

"Right."

Roberto was hoping Block would object to the relevancy of this testimony, but Block did not take the bait. Roberto had told him during the discovery period of the fact that Julieta would be called to testify and of the nature of her testimony, as was the obligation of the defense, so Block knew that by objecting he would make it possible for Roberto to explain why she was there and, although Roberto was not under oath, his words would have an impact on the jury. Block was not about to give him that chance.

"Do you live with your husband?" asked Roberto.

"No, sir, we are separated but not divorced."

The Judge glanced at Block, expecting him to object, Block looked away.

"Where were you married?"

Before Julieta could answer, much to Block's dismay and Roberto's satisfaction, the Judge asked Roberto, "Where are we going with this testimony, Mr. Duran?"

Roberto felt he could have jumped to the ceiling by the chance, but he only stood up and said, "Your Honor, I know this seems irrelevant to the case, but we believe we can prove that it was her husband who placed the cocaine in Mr. Pardo's luggage as revenge."

Judges know nothing of a case before the trial, so the Judge understood that he had fallen for Roberto's subtle trap. He only smiled slightly and said, "Very well, if the prosecutor does not object—"

"The prosecutor does object strenuously, Your Honor," said Block standing up. "And we would request an instruction to the jury that what Mr. Duran just said is not evidence, that Mr. Duran is not under oath."

"I'm sure that the members of the jury remember my opening instructions that what the attorneys say is not evidence only what a witness says under oath is evidence," said the Judge in effect giving the requested instruction although seeming not to do it. The Judge turned to Roberto, "What is your response to the objection, Mr. Duran?"

"Your Honor, it was necessary for me to ask these irrelevant questions to put Mrs. Velasco's testimony in context. I will go into the relevant portion right away."

"Very well, objection overruled, go ahead Mr. Duran."

"I'll ask again, Mrs. Velasco, where were you married?"

"In Havana, Cuba."

"Mrs. Velasco, what is your estranged husband's occupation?"

"He is a drug-trafficker."

There was a hush going through the courtroom at the sound of these words. Roberto asked, "How do you know this?" He crossed his fingers waiting for the answer they had rehearsed.

"Because I went through the papers in his office and saw several things that confirmed that he was a drug baron, as I had been suspecting for some time." What she had said was of her personal knowledge and therefore could not be objected to as hearsay.

"Did Cesar and you have any children?"

"One daughter only," she said with a tone of sadness. Roberto, who knew her story, could easily understand.

"Is your daughter still alive?"

"No, sir, she committed suicide after breaking with your client, Manolo Pardo. She was pregnant."

Manolo's face was gray and empty at these words. Several jurors could not avoid turning to look at him.

"Was your husband affected by her death?"

"Very much so, he swore he would get revenge," said Julieta.

"Objection, hearsay, Your Honor," said Block, who was just waiting for the chance to object now that Roberto had gotten away with his trick.

"Mr. Duran?" said the Judge.

"We do not know why Mrs. Velasco is saying this, Your Honor, but assuming it was because her husband told her, it could presumably fall into an exception to the hearsay rule," responded Roberto.

"Overruled," said the Judge, "But establish the basis for her knowledge, Mr. Duran."

"I will, Your Honor." Turning to the witness, Roberto asked, "Mrs. Velasco, how and when did your husband swear revenge against my client?"

"He called less than one hour after my daughter's body was found, I have no idea how he found out about the suicide, he seems to have eyes everywhere, and he shouted on the telephone that he would have Manolo pay for it."

"It is hearsay, Your Honor," objected Block.

"Your Honor," said Roberto, "Clearly the statement falls within the 'then existing mental condition' exception to the hearsay rule. Mrs. Velasco just testified that her husband called shortly after her daughter's death and shouted on the phone. It is sufficient to show that the declarant intended to do harm to Manolo. In the alternative, it would be the 'excited utterance' exception."

"Objection overruled," said the Judge. "Please continue, Mr. Duran."

"Yes Your Honor," said Roberto, and turned to the witness. "Mrs. Velasco, do you believe your husband actually carried out his threat?"

"Objection, that would be speculation," said Block.

"Sustained."

Roberto was a little disappointed, but he was fully expecting the objection, Block was an experienced litigator. Now he decided it would be better to leave the direct questioning at that point.

"Pass the witness, Your Honor."

"I believe this is a good time for our morning recess, see you in fifteen minutes," said the Judge.

24

JULIETA'S CROSS-EXAMINATION

Back from the morning recess, the Judge, turning to the prosecutor, asked, "Mr. Block?"

"A few questions, Your Honor," responded Block and turned to the witness, "Mrs. Velasco, counsel for the defense just asked you if you believed that your husband carried out his threat against the defendant in this case, Mr. Manuel Pardo. I objected as speculation. What Mr. Duran did not ask you is if you have personal knowledge of your husband *actually* carrying out his threat. Please tell the jury if you know for a fact that your husband set a trap for Mr. Pardo?" asked Block in his typical convoluted way.

"No, I do not have any personal knowledge of that."

"Aha. Then you simply surmise that it was your husband who placed the cocaine in the defendant's bags to carry out his threat."

"I guess you could say so," answered Julieta.

Having advised Block of the nature of Julieta's testimony, as was his duty, Roberto knew that Block would stress the speculative nature of her testimony. If it had been Roberto, he would have left the cross-examination at that point. But Roberto was hoping that Block would then try to discredit Julieta's testimony even more by going into a very lengthy cross-examination as was his custom. Roberto was not wrong.

"You stated that you knew for a fact that your husband is a drug trafficker, is that right?"

"Yes."

"Did you know that when you married him?"

"No, of course not?"

"What did you believe him to be?"

"I knew that he was a political sciences professor, a highly dedicated and idealistic individual," responded Julieta vehemently.

"That was in Cuba, when you married him?"

"Yes, sir."

"Was he a communist?"

"Objection, Your Honor, that is irrelevant," said Roberto standing up.

"What's the relevancy, Mr. Block?" asked the Judge.

"I'll go into something different, Your Honor."

"Mrs. Velasco, during Mr. Duran's questions you answered that you had married in Cuba, is that correct?"

"Yes, sir."

"Did you continue to live in Cuba?"

"No, sir. Shortly after our marriage Cesar and I, my husband and I, went to live in Mexico City. That is where I live now."

"Yes. And what did your husband do for a living in Mexico City?"

"He was also a political sciences professor, but at the National University of Mexico."

"I see. What year was that?'

"1977."

"Was your daughter born then?"

"No, my daughter was born in 1984."

"So you had not separated from your husband then until after 1984, is that correct?"

"No, sir, it is not correct. I separated from my husband in 1979."

"I do not understand, how could you have a daughter with your husband if you were separated?" The tone of voice of Block was showing the protestant puritan he was, a little shocked by the situation.

"It is a long story, sir."

"I would like to hear it," responded Block. Roberto felt like jumping with joy. It was once more that Block, trying to discredit Julieta, was giving the defense a chance to bring up testimony that would have been considered totally irrelevant if asked during the direct examination.

"Well, sir, my husband disappeared in the year of 1979. One day he never returned from his job at the National University of Mexico. About three months later we, his parents and I, received a report that he had been killed by the Mexican Army while leading an uprising of peasants in the State of Chiapas, in the Southwest of the Republic of Mexico."

"So, obviously that man was not the father of your daughter?" Block was genuinely curious now.

"That is not correct. That man was the father of my daughter Julieta."

"I am sorry ma-ma, but I do not understand," said Block with a look of genuine confusion.

"It is kind of complicated, but... may I explain?" said Julieta sounding like a small child and turning to the Judge.

"Please do," responded the Judge, who was obviously taken by the beauty of the witness.

"Right after we came from Cuba, I had started working as an assistant for my father-in-law. He's a Certified Public Accountant and I wanted to become one too. When I became certified, my father-in-law hired me as an associate in his office."

"Your Honor, all this is totally irrelevant," objected Block.

"You asked her to please explain, Mr. Block, I believe that is what she is trying to do," ruled the Judge who then turned to Julieta and said with a reassuring smile: "Please continue ma-am."

"Yes, sir. A couple of years later, in 1983, I was made a partner. Shortly after, our office received a call from the San Cristobal Sugar Mill that they wanted to see me. My father-in-law was overjoyed, San Cristobal was a very large company."

The Judge nodded and everybody in the courtroom was hanging from her words, although Roberto was a little worried that the testimony was proceeding in the form of a narrative, rather than question and answer, but if nobody objected, so be it.

"There had been rumors that the mill was nearly bankrupt. Then it was purchased by a group of investors. I assumed that the investors were American and the reason they wanted to meet with me, instead of with my father-in-law, was because I am fluent in English and he is not."

"And that was the reason?" asked the Judge.

"No, it was not. San Cristobal Mill is in the town of the same name, about a two-hour drive from Mexico City. I traveled there. After arriving I visited with the Comptroller for a while and learned that his group was made up of South American investors and the President of the company wanted to see me," she said, avoiding, just as Roberto had instructed her, the possibility of a hearsay objection.

"I was taken to the office of the President and it surprised me to notice that the offices had been redecorated very elegantly, which was strange if it was true that the company was in bad financial shape," she continued, "I was shown into the private suite of the President. It was the size of an apartment and very plush. It had a wide window overlooking the sugar cane fields and when the Comptroller and I walked in, the man was sitting looking through the window with his back to the door by which we had walked in. The only thing I could see was the top of a blond head."

"And then?" asked the Judge, curious as a cat and who had seemed to take over the questioning.

"The President turned slowly around on his high-backed chair with a theatrical air and I almost fainted as he began to laugh. It was Cesar, my husband. He dispatched the Comptroller out of the office and after we were alone I learned that he had not been killed in Chiapas as everyone had thought." she responded, again avoiding any hearsay objection.

"Go ahead Mr. Block, continue your questioning," said the Judge, finally aware of the narrative form.

"You mean to say that after a disappearance of several years, let me see..." Block was not very good with numbers. "From 79 through 83, I guess, four years. After four years of being presumed dead, he reappeared all of a sudden?"

"Yes, sir that is exactly what happened."

"And you decided to take him back?" asked Block, again with his puritanical tone.

"I had no choice, I was still very much in love with him." Her answer stroke a chord in those in attendance and Roberto could see sympathy reflected in the eyes of the jurors.

"So it was then that your child was born?"

"That's right. Almost one year later."

"So, how did you find out that the man was a drug-trafficker?" asked Block.

"I learned that after fleeing Mexico, Cesar had gone to Peru where apparently he had made a fortune dealing with sugar cane. During those dealings he had found out that San Cristobal was in bad shape and, missing me and being lonely for Mexico, or so he said, he had bought the company and here he was."

"Again, when did you find out that your husband was a drug trafficker, as you allege?"

"I began suspecting it because Cesar did actually had me working as an accountant because he did not want his father to know he was alive."

"How strange. Did he say why?"

"No, he didn't, and I didn't ask, I simply assumed that it had to do with his ideology change. In Cuba, Cesar had been an idealist, now he was only concerned with how much money he could make."

"But, when did you confirm your suspicions about your husband, as you say?"

"As the person in charge of auditing I soon discovered that San Cristobal was broke. The only reason it kept solvent was because it received every month a series of capital investments from Cesar as its only real shareholder."

"And that is what according to you confirmed your suspicions?" the voice of Block indicated how flimsy he considered the evidence.

"No, sir, but Cesar's lifestyle was extravagantly luxurious, at the time San Cristobal required about a million dollars every month to break even."

"Was that enough to confirm your suspicions?"

"No, sir."

"Well, ma-am, I would appreciate it if you finally tell me how you confirmed your suspicions," Block wanted to sound exasperated, but he actually sounded interested.

"It was one night. We were both asleep in our bedroom in the big plantation house that Cesar had ordered rebuilt when the phone rang and Cesar answered, he listened for a short while responding just with a short 'yes' or 'no.' It was clear that he was very upset when he slammed the phone down. After that, he called Victor, the Comptroller and ordered him to have all the people come over to the house immediately."

"And?"

"Before leaving, he said that there had been trouble with one of the trucks which carried the sugar that San Cristobal exported to the United States --"

"Objection, hearsay," interrupted Block standing up, while Julieta looked confused.

"Mr. Duran?" asked the Judge.

"Your Honor, the statement of the witness does not have the purpose of showing the truth of what her husband said, only that he did say it. In fact, I suspect that what her husband said was not the truth," responded Roberto.

"Overruled, please continue, Mrs. Velasco."

"Thank you sir," said Julieta before continuing, "I was really surprised and curious, I could not help it, after Cesar had been away for ten minutes or so, I went downstairs to the music room that was next to his studio-library, where they were all meeting. They were talking about a truck that had 'fallen.' Then I discovered that Cesar had been using the shipments of sugar from San Cristobal to the United States to conceal cocaine."

"That is a big leap, ma-am, from words that a truck had fallen to conclude that it had to do with cocaine shipments. It could be that the truck had fallen into a ravine, could it not?" Block sounded flustered.

"Objection, argumentative," said Roberto.

"Ask questions, Mr. Block, don't argue with the witness," ruled the Judge.

"I'm sorry, Your Honor." Turning to Julieta, Block said, "You will agree that the word fallen has nothing to do with cocaine?"

"Yes, sir, but it was not just that word, I was looking through the keyhole and saw on the conference table a clear plastic bag with cocaine and my husband was saying that it could not be a coincidence that U.S. Customs had discovered the stuff, and pointed to the bag–."

"Ms. Velasco, did you perform a test to determine that the substance you saw in the bag was in fact cocaine?" interrupted Block.

"No, I did not."

"May we approach the bench, Your Honor?" Asked Block.

"Go ahead."

"Your Honor, at this time the Government moves for a mistrial. The testimony about a bag of cocaine is highly prejudicial. The jury has obviously been prejudiced by Ms. Velasco's testimony of something that may not be cocaine, but baby powder," whispered Block once at the bench.

"Your Honor, the prosecutor has not asked Ms. Velasco if she had any other way of knowing, other than performing a test, if the bag in fact contained cocaine," countered Roberto.

"Are you planning to ask her, Roberto?" Asked the Judge, informally using the first name, as he did in private.

"Absolutely, Judge, and I believe that she will answer that she saw them snorting from the bag. Nobody snorts baby powder, that I know," said Roberto with a festive tone.

"For the record, the Government's motion for mistrial is denied, go ahead gentlemen," ruled the Judge.

Both went back to their tables. Block, who had remained up, was silent for a few seconds then said, "No more questions."

It was clear that Block felt that Julieta's testimony had been damaging and decided to exercise some damage control by stopping at her admission.

"Very well, it is already pretty late," said the Judge looking at his watch, "Ladies and gentleman of the jury, I will see you tomorrow to start at 9 a.m. promptly and remember all my instructions," said the Judge.

25

MANOLO TAKES THE STAND

Thursday morning, once the jury members were all seated, the Judge turned to Roberto and said, "The prosecutor passed the witness yesterday, do you have any redirect, Mr. Duran?"

"Yes, Your Honor, a few questions to clarify the cross-examination of the Prosecutor," said Roberto, glancing at Block, who just looked the other way.

Addressing Julieta, Roberto asked, "Before we recessed yesterday, Mrs. Velasco, you were saying that you saw your husband pointing to a bag which contained a white powdery substance that you assumed to be cocaine, right?"

"Yes."

"Why did you assume it was cocaine?"

"Because, shortly before Cesar made his comment and pointed to the bag, I had seen some of the others remove powder from the little bag and, using a razor blade, make long lines and start snorting them."

"Objection, Your Honor, it is speculation," said Block, standing up.

"Overruled. The jury can make their own minds and decide if they believe it was cocaine or not," ruled the Judge.

"You told us in answer to one of my direct questions that you had personally seen documents that demonstrated that your husband is a drug trafficker"

"That is correct, yes."

"How was it that you discovered those?"

"After I saw the cocaine and heard Cesar's comments, I returned to my room and made believe that I was sound asleep. After a while, Cesar came back to wake me up and tell me that he had to leave immediately to travel to the United States. He was away for three days,"

"So more or less you had the house all to yourself?"

"Pretty much, yes."

"What did you do?"

"Cesar had left in a hurry, so he did not close his personal safe, of which nobody else had the combination. I guess he must have thought he had, but he did not turn the wheel. I was down in his studio for a long time going over his papers but did not find anything special. Then, I went to the painting that had his safe behind it because underneath his safe was my safe, where I had the jewels he had been giving me. I wanted to put them all away, I did not feel like using them again after what I suspected. Almost by accident, I touched the door of his safe and noticed that it was open."

"Did you go into the safe?"

"Yes, I did."

"What did you find?"

"A ledger that contained a detailed description of all his drug dealings. He was not dealing only with cocaine, but also with marihuana and heroine. The ledger described transactions of over 300 million dollars. Then I understood that San Cristobal was only a front and why Cesar was able to continue funding the bankrupt sugar mill."

"What did you do next?"

"When he came back after three days, I told him that I knew everything, but that I would not tell anybody because I was carrying his baby, just that I did not want anything more to do with him," she said.

"How did he react?"

"He did not like it, but I guess he still cared enough for me not to do me any harm."

"Did you consider contacting the authorities?"

"I did consider it. It would have been useless. In Mexico Cesar was, at least at that time, virtually untouchable. He had contacts very high in the government and I do not believe he would have been prosecuted. The only consequence of filing a complaint would have been to enrage him and risk being killed," she responded in a matter-of-fact voice. The testimony clearly impressed everybody in the courtroom.

"After your child was born did you see him again?"

"Occasionally. Cesar bought a house for me and for my daughter, whose name was Julieta also. About one year after I left San Cristobal, there was a press release stating that the mill had been sold because the American investors who owned it had lost faith in the country. It was typical of Cesar and his hatred for America. I never again knew where Cesar was, he would visit young Julieta and me about once a month for an hour or so. Always at strange hours and always following a telephone call from him or one of his many assistants saying that he was coming."

"Do you know if Cesar and your daughter Julieta continued having a relationship?"

"Yes, very much so, in fact Julieta became pretty close to her father on her own. I did not object, he may be a monster but he was still her father."

"I understand, pass the witness, Your Honor."

"Any re-cross Mr. Block?"

"No, Judge."

After Julieta left the stand Roberto called the name of the first character witness. It was a relatively short testimony of a Houston banker who testified that he knew the family very well and that they were very honorable and highly respected in banking circles all over the world.

The prosecutor cross-examined with questions pointing to the fact that the witness's opinion might change if he were to learn that Manolo was in fact trafficking drugs. It was the typical cross-examination to try to show for the jury that the witness could have a very positive concept of the defendant but that he might be mistaken.

After the witness was excused the Judge said, "Let's take our morning recess. Have your next witness ready when we come back, Mr. Duran."

After the recess the next two witnesses were an almost identical replay of the first character witness, both as to the direct examination and the typical lengthy cross by Block. By the time the second witness finished it was noon and the Judge sent everybody to lunch.

———

Back from lunch, Roberto called the name of a prominent Houston surgeon who had traveled to Houston from Mexico City on the same flight as Manolo Pardo and had witnessed the arrest. Bobby Cavazos, Roberto's private investigator, had as usual made a homerun with this witness because the surgeon was very well-known and pretty upset and disgusted by how rough the agents had been to Manolo during the arrest and stated it so in very clear terms.

Contrary to his custom, Block only asked one question for cross-examination, "Doctor, the agents really had no way of knowing if Mr. Pardo would become violent when arrested, is that true?"

"I guess they didn't, but I still feel they did not have to be so harsh," was the answer.

"Pass the witness," said Block.

"Mr. Duran, any redirect?"

"No, Your Honor, Dr. Gidley may be excused. The defense now calls Mr. Manuel Pardo to the stand."

There was electricity in the courtroom when Manolo walked to the stand and took the oath from the case manager. Roberto, observing the jurors, felt that they were not unsympathetic to Manolo.

After asking Manolo to give his full name for the record, Roberto, just as he had done during the detention hearing said, "I just have one more question, Mr. Pardo. Did you know there was cocaine in the bags when you were sent to the inspection area in the George Bush Intercontinental Airport?"

"No sir, I had no idea that there was anything in them other than my clothes and personal effects."

"Pass the witness, your Honor," said Roberto.

Block, who had been surprised by Roberto calling his client during the detention hearing, was better prepared for a cross-examination this time. "Are you really asking the jury to believe that you did not know that you had cocaine in your bags?"

"Those were not my bags," responded Manolo firmly, "My bags did not have anything else than my clothes and personal effects as I just said."

"But you will agree with me that the bags inspected contained your clothes, yes or no?

"Somebody must have changed my clothes," responded Manolo.

"I will ask you again. It is a yes or no answer. Did those bags contain your clothes and personal effects, yes or no?"

"Yes, someone must have changed–"

"Objection, non-responsive after 'yes'. I ask that the jury be instructed to disregard any answer after his 'yes'," interrupted Block.

"Sustained. The jury will disregard what the witness said after answering 'yes'."

Block got up and, after requesting the Judge's permission, approached the witness with a blue Continental ticket jacket in his hand. "Let me show you this ticket jacket, Mr. Pardo, do you recognize it?"

"I believe it is the jacket that was given to me when I documented my bags in Mexico City."

"Exactly. Your Honor, the government offers exhibit seventeen."

"Any objections Mr. Duran?" asked the Judge, after Block had approached Roberto and shown him the jacket.

"No objection."

"Government's Exhibit seventeen is admitted," ruled the Judge.

"Do you see these slips affixed to the jacket, Mr. Pardo?"

"Yes, sir."

"Will you read the numbers?"

Manolo read the identifying numbers.

Block then produced the indictment in the case and handed it to Manolo. "Will you please read the numbers of the tags that were attached to the bags you presented for inspection at the airport?"

Manolo read the numbers again for the jury.

Turning to face the jury, Block asked, "Are those numbers the same as the slips affixed to your jacket?"

"Yes they are, but I don't know— "

"Just answer my question, Mr. Pardo, are those the same numbers as the slips affixed to your ticket's jacket, yes or no?"

"Yes."

"The bags inspected did contain cocaine in them, you yourself saw the cocaine when the inspector cut the lining, yes or no?"

"Yes."

"You are still contending that you did not know there was cocaine in your bags when you checked them at Mexico City's airport?"

"There was no cocaine in the bags I checked in Mexico City."

"But the bags you submitted for inspection did have these tag numbers that coincide with those slips on your ticket's jacket?" asked Block.

"Yes it is the same number, but—"

"I pass the witness," stated Block, interrupting Manolo.

"Redirect, Mr. Duran?" asked the Judge.

Roberto, who had suspected what the cross was going to be, also suspected how Block planned to rebut the testimony of his client. He just answered, "No redirect, Your Honor."

"Call your next witness, Mr. Duran."

"The defense rests."

"I guess we will take our afternoon recess," said the Judge.

26

REBUTTAL

B ack from the afternoon recess, the Judge said:
"Any rebuttal, Mr. Block?"

"The government calls Mr. Alexander Simpson, an employee of Continental Airlines who is in charge of luggage control for the airline."

Simpson took the stand and, under Block's direct, stated how secure the tagging system was and how difficult it would be to take off a tag affixed to any bag and affix it to another without it being noticed. It was a lengthy and complicated technical explanation. When Block passed the witness Roberto could see that the jurors were looking at him, like challenging him to try to convince them that it would have been possible for someone to have changed those bags.

Roberto, who had rehearsed this moment, took a deep breath, stood up, requested permission to do so and approached the witness. He knew that this was a critical moment in the trial and knew also that his cross could not be very powerful, so he had decided he had to compensate with a little theatrical drama.

Pulling his billfold from the right rear pocket of his trousers, Roberto opened it and extracted three one-hundred dollar bills, which he placed in front of Simpson. "Will you please tell the jury what these are?"

"Three bills of one hundred dollars," replied Simpson.

In a jury trial both sides always know what exhibits are going to be produced by the other side. The court rules require a list of exhibits to be exchanged before the trial. One exception is rebuttal evidence. Because one side can never be sure that there is a need to rebut the testimony of the other, the rules allow for previously undisclosed witnesses and evidence to be produced at the rebuttal's witness direct or cross-examination. So Block had no idea of what Roberto had planned.

Roberto walked back to the defense table and picked up a folder and approached the witness again. "Will you please examine the three bills, Mr. Simpson?"

Simpson examined them, looked at Roberto, and said, "Yes?"

"Do you notice anything strange?"

"No," answered Simpson, examining them once more.

"Let me show you what I have marked for identification purposes only as defense exhibit nine, will you please read what it says on the top?"

"United States Treasury, Certificate of Authenticity" responded Simpson.

"Your Honor, I am showing this document to the prosecutor and request that it be admitted."

Block, approaching the stand, looked at the document and said, "No objection, Your Honor."

"Admitted," ruled the Judge.

"Now, Mr. Simpson, this is really a Certificate of Counterfeit because what it says is that one of the bills that I have handed you is not authentic U.S. currency, isn't that correct?" asked Roberto showing the witness the relevant portion.

"That is what it says, yes, that bill number..." and he stated the number, "...is in fact a counterfeit of a true United States currency obligation."

"Objection, relevancy, Your Honor," stated Block.

"The relevancy will be apparent in a minute Judge," countered Roberto.

"Overruled," said the Judge.

"You will agree with me that the United States Government uses very stringent safeguards to insure that U.S. currency not be counterfeited, right"

Absolutely," answered Simpson.

"Yet, would you please read for the ladies and gentlemen of the jury what the Certificate of Authenticity states here," said Roberto pointing to defense exhibit nine.

"It says that this bill was seized together with many other bills from Colombian drug cartel members who are suspected of having counterfeited them."

"Does Continental Airlines use safeguards as stringent to produce the tags that are attached to the luggage as those used to produce currency?'

"Objection, speculation," said Block.

"If he knows, Your Honor," countered Roberto.

"Overruled."

"Please answer, if you know," said Roberto.

"I don't know for sure."

"I will ask you this way, will you agree with me that if cartel members have the expertise to counterfeit currency of the United States, it is likely that they may also have found a way to take your airline's tags off from a piece of luggage and fasten them to another piece?"

"Objection, this again calls for speculation," said Block.

"The witness is an expert in airline document security, he may give an opinion with respect to that," countered Roberto. Fact witnesses can never give an opinion on the evidence, but expert witnesses are allowed, and in fact frequently called, to state their opinions on the evidence

"Overruled," said the Judge, "You yourself have offered him as an expert in baggage documents, Mr. Block."

"Answer please," said Roberto to Simpson.

"I guess that is possible, yes."

"No more questions."

"Any redirect, Mr. Block."

"No, Your Honor, the Government closes."

The Judge turned to Roberto, who stood up and was about to announce that the defense closed when Luis Gil touched his arm. Roberto turned and saw Luis pointing to the door of the courtroom. Roberto looked at the door and could see Lupe Saldaña standing at the door of the courtroom.

Instead of closing, Roberto turned to the Judge and stated that he needed to approach the bench.

Both Block and Roberto approached the Judge and Roberto said, "Judge I just saw a man walk into the courtroom who may be bringing me newly discovered evidence in the case, I request a recess to speak with him,"

"Mr. Block?"

"This is highly irregular Judge, I have no idea who this mysterious witness is."

"Mr. Duran?"

"In fact Mr. Guadalupe Saldaña is listed as a witness, if the prosecutor reads his list. Only that I listed him as a possible rebuttal witness."

"Rebuttal for what?" stated Block.

"It will not be a rebuttal witness, I believe this is newly discovered evidence, Your Honor."

"Well, let's break for the day and we will have a short conference tomorrow morning outside of the presence of the jury," decided the Judge.

The next day, Friday morning, the Judge walked into the court-room and called the case after giving instructions to the officer in charge of the jury not to bring the jurors in yet. The courtroom was empty because Roberto, with Block's acquiescence, had requested the Judge to seal the courtroom. Seal the courtroom means that all persons, other than essential court personnel, the parties, their attorneys and in this case the investigators for the defense and the government, are asked to step out and wait outside because the hearing taking place requires the utmost secrecy.

"So what about this new witness, Mr. Duran?" said the Judge.

"Your Honor, Mr. Saldaña is a supervisory agent of the D.E.A. that has discovered evidence connected with the case that confirms what we suspected, but did not know for sure."

"What is the evidence?"

"Mr. Saldaña will testify that a man confessed to having placed the cocaine in bags that were then exchanged at the airport, before my client went through Customs."

"That is hearsay, Your Honor," objected Block.

"It is Mr. Duran. Or does it fall within one of the exceptions?"

"Yes, Your Honor. It's an admission against penal interest. The man could have been be prosecuted for this crime."

"In that case, did Mr. Saldaña give the man his 'Miranda' warnings?" retorted Block.

"He did," responded Roberto.

"You said, 'could have been', why?" Asked the Judge.

"Because he was killed in the process of giving his statement."

"Then it may also be considered a dying declaration?" asked the Judge, thinking of yet another exception to the hearsay rule.

"No, Your Honor, the man was killed while he was giving the statement but he did not know he was going to be killed. The statement was videotaped," responded Roberto.

"Well, at the very least you have greatly piqued my curiosity," said the Judge. "I guess we need to see the tape outside the presence of the jury. Are you ready to authenticate the tape?"

"Yes, Your Honor."

"Go ahead."

"The defense calls Mr. Guadalupe Saldaña."

Lupe was called in, took the oath, sat on the witness stand and Roberto asked him, "Will you give us your full name, and please spell it for the court reporter."

Lupe answered and spelled his name and then Roberto said, "Mr. Saldaña, you asked me to request from His Honor that the courtroom be sealed so that you could give your testimony in the greatest privacy possible, is that right?"

Lupe answered, "Yes sir, that is correct."

"Will you please explain to the Court what is your occupation and why is it that you requested such a thing?" continued Roberto.

"I am a Senior Supervisory Special Agent with the Drug Enforcement Administration. Also, I am the highest official said agency has in the Republic of Mexico. My work, of necessity because it is in a foreign country, has to be undercover. I pretend to be a drug baron in Mexico. If my identity were known, all my organization and, of course, my life would be in grave danger," answered Lupe, with a very matter-of-fact voice.

"Thank you very much sir," replied Roberto. Then, turning to the Judge, he said, "Your Honor, I would request your approval to lead my own witness in order to fully develop a factual basis for his testimony."

"Very well, go ahead," replied the Judge after looking toward Block who had stood up and shaken his head indicating, 'no objection.'

"During the investigation of this case, Commander Luis Gil, seated at the defense table as one of my investigators, and I, asked you to investigate certain facts that had to do with this case, right?"

"Right, and I did discover, through a tip from one of my informants, the presence of a witness very material to this case," was Lupe's reply.

"And the information was beneficial to your agency, so you did not waste the resources of the D.E.A. in something private, or did you?"

"Absolutely not. I have been after the organization my informant was working on for years. Anything that we learn about it benefits the D.E.A."

"Going back to your informant, without telling us what he told you, could you please tell the Court what was it that you found out?" asked Roberto.

"That a man who seemed to have participated in this case was hiding out in El Salvador because he was fearful for his life. The information stated also that the man was apparently dead broke and would be willing to exchange information for money. I contacted the man through my agents, offered him one hundred thousand dollars, that you volunteered to provide me with--"

"When you say 'you volunteered' you are talking of my client and his family, is that right?" interrupted Roberto.

"Yes sir, your client's grandfather offered to, and did in fact give me that money," replied Lupe, who continued, "After that, I traveled to San Salvador, the capital of El Salvador, got in contact with the man, through the resident agent of the D.E.A., and he agreed to come over to our hotel and give a statement."

"What happened next?"

"On this past Tuesday, I had arranged for a conference room, and a video recorder at the Camino Real of San Salvador. It is one of the top hotels in the city and very centrally located, so it would be easy to have surveillance and security. The man had agreed to show up at 8:00 in the morning."

"Did he show up?"

"No, he did not, so after it was past 11:00 and he had not showed, I started to try and find out what was going on--"

"Allow me to interrupt you again," asked Roberto, "Why did you wait until eleven?"

"People in Latin American countries live on a different schedule, when they say 8:00, it may mean, 9:00 or 10:00 or even later, so I allowed extra time for that eventuality," was Lupe's reply.

"Very well, sorry to have interrupted you. What happened next," asked Roberto.

"Afterwards I located him, and to make a long story short, we ended up having to go to his house at almost 8:00 p.m. that evening. His house is way up on the sides of one of the hills that surround San Salvador. The road up, although it is in the city, looks more like the bed of a dry river. In fact, the locals say that it turns into a river every time it rains hard."

"After locating the house," asked Roberto, "Did you take a videotaped statement of the man?"

"Yes sir, in a house which is about the size of this box," answered Lupe, pointing to the empty jury box.

Roberto stood up and asked, "May I approach the witness, Your Honor?"

"Yes," said the Judge.

"Mr. Saldaña, I hand you what has been marked, for purposes of identification only, as defendant's exhibit number ten," said Roberto looking at his list where the exhibits introduced during the direct examination of the prior witnesses were recorded. "Do you recognize what this is and will you tell the Court what it is," he finished, handing Lupe a videotape cassette.

"This is the tape of the statement I took this past Tuesday evening," replied Lupe, and gave the date.

"How can you be sure it is?" asked Roberto.

"Because it has a label that I personally placed on it with my initials. Also, the plastic cover has a little carving that I myself made to be able to identify it even if the label is pulled off," responded Lupe.

"Your Honor, at this time I offer into evidence defendant's ten," said Roberto.

Block stood up and said, "I don't think chain of custody has been established, Your Honor."

The Judge seemed pretty annoyed by the objection. He turned to Saldaña and asked him, "You have had this videotape in your personal possession ever since you taped the statement that you are testifying about, is that correct?"

"Yes, Your Honor," replied Lupe.

"Defendant's ten is admitted," said the Judge.

"At this time, Your Honor, I would like to play it for the Court," offered Roberto.

"Very well, let's make a ten minute recess while you set up the equipment," said the Judge.

27

THE MAN IN EL SALVADOR

A fter the recess the Judge said:
    "Go ahead."

"By the way sir, before playing the tape I will ask you, did you need an interpreter to take the statement?" asked Roberto.

"No sir, because of what will become apparent on the cassette itself," replied Lupe.

Roberto punched the 'on' button and the T.V. came on showing the picture of a room that, as Lupe had stated, seemed to be about half the size of the jury box. On one corner of the small room was a television set that was on and showed the same scene of the set in the courtroom, reproduced ad infinitum. Next, was a man staring at the T.V. set and making a comment in Spanish about the fact that he was on T.V., while he laughed and looked silly.

Then, a voice that Roberto instantly recognized as the voice of Lupe, asked in English, "What's your name?"

"I will say Pablo Gomez, but who cares," answered the man with a very thick accent and a coarse laugh at the end.

"Pablo, I'm going to read you from this card what your rights are before asking you any question, you understand?"

"Yes, you explains to me before, no matters."

"But you do understand these are your rights"

"Yes, no matters," said the man again in very poor English.

Saldaña then proceeded on the tape to read all the Miranda warnings asking the man after each one if he understood it. After each and every one of them the man answered "Yes I do. No matters."

"Pablo, I understand you were part of an organization that trafficked in cocaine all over Europe, Central America, Mexico and the United States, right?" asked the voice of Lupe.

"Yes, it is the biggest and more powerful of all," answered the man with pride in his voice.

"About four months ago did something happen that forced you to leave the organization?" asked Lupe's voice.

"Yes," said the man with a stupid smile on his face, "The boss, he got angry at me, he wanted to kill me."

"Is that right?" asked Lupe's voice.

"Yes, he said to kill me, but nobody finds me, nobody can kill me," said the man, finishing again with a coarse laugh.

"Pablo," continued the voice of Lupe, "You told a friend of mine that you need money because you spent all you made, that you are broke and, in exchange for money that may allow you to live the rest of your life, you are willing to tell me about a special work you did for the boss, is that correct?"

"Yes, I need money. I have no money," said the man.

"Have I have given you money to tell us your story?" asked Lupe's voice.

"Yes, one hundred thousand dollars, here it is," replied the man, caressing a briefcase that was standing next to him.

"Come on Pablo, show the money to us," asked Lupe's voice.

The man fumbled with the locks of the briefcase and finally opened it and showed, with great pride, a large number of bills, seemingly fifty-dollar each, bundled together with rubber bands inside the briefcase.

"Now Pablo, what did I tell you when I gave you the money?" asked Lupe's voice.

"That you wanted true and only the true. Not to tell lies or invent. That money was mine to keep, but you wanted the true," responded the man in his thick-accented and terrible English.

"Very well Pablo," continued Lupe's voice, "Now, tell us what did you do to the boss to make him want to kill you?"

"You want me to tell you about the bags and the rich kid, or what I did with them?" asked the man who obviously was as dumb as he appeared to be.

"I want you to start from the beginning and tell us the whole story," was saying Lupe's voice patiently.

"Well, I was in Houston, and the boss ordered me to go to the airport and make a switch."

"Which airport and what is a switch?" asked Lupe's voice.

"The big one, Intercontinental it's called," said the man.

"Intercontinental and also George Bush, right?" interjected Lupe's voice.

"Yes, that one," said the man, "There in the airport switch the bags."

"What is switching the bags," insisted Lupe's voice.

"To change the ones the boss had given to us for the bags that the rich kid had checked into the flight," said the man.

"Was that the first time you switched bags?" asked the voice of Lupe.

"No, we do it all the time, the boss had me working in Houston because I speak English and I got job in airport and always switched the bags of our people," said the man.

"Why then do we still arrest people in the airport who are carrying cocaine in their bags?" asked Lupe's voice, pretending to be confused.

"Competitors," answered the man.

"You mean to say that the men of your boss are never

captured, that those who are caught in the airport are competitors of your boss?" asked the voice of Lupe.

"Exactly," answered the man.

"So what do you do when one of your people arrives carrying bags full of cocaine?" asked the voice of Lupe.

"We switch them for other bags that only have clothes and we take away the ones that have cocaine and get them out of the airport by the black door... as the gringos say," ended the man with a laugh.

"You mean 'back door'?"

"Yes, yes, back door, back door."

"This time what did you do?"

"The opposite, changed the bags that had cocaine for bags that did not have."

"What about the clothes that were in the real bags?" asked Lupe's voice.

"I changed them. I took them from the real bags and put them into the switch bags, easy!" answered the man cockily.

"What about the switch bags?" was asking the voice of Lupe, adopting the terminology of the man. "Who gave you those bags?"

"The boss sent them. But they were empty, they only had the pockets in the sides, prepared to fill them with cocaine," answered the man.

"Where did you get the cocaine?"

"Ah... that was the big mess," answered the man, with a tone of regret in his voice.

"What do you mean?" asked the voice of Lupe.

"Well, the boss tells me, 'Pancho, fill the pockets of these bags with cocaine—" Block stood up, asked Roberto to turn off the tape and objected, "Your Honor, I object to the hearsay nature of what the man is stating that his boss told him."

"It's not being admitted to prove the truth of what the boss told the man, Your Honor, just that he said it," responded Roberto.

"Overruled," said the Judge and ordered that the tape be rewound a little before turning it on.

Roberto turned it on and the man on the T.V. said, "Well, the boss tells me, 'Pancho, fill the pockets of these bags with cocaine from the last shipment you received,' I say, 'Yes boss, I will do,'" said the man without realizing that he had just given away his real first name. "Then, I think, why use cocaine so valuable? Why not use some of the coke we have ready to sell on the streets, cocaine that is cut down and less valuable. No one will ever know. This rich kid the boss wants to fuck up will go to jail and nobody will know. I can keep the difference in the price and prepare my nest, you know, for my retirement," finished the man, again with a lugubrious laugh.

"Did the boss find out?" asked Lupe's voice.

"Yes," replied the man with dismay, "That is when I had to run away and—"

The videotape was suddenly cut off and the T.V. screen filled with falling snow. Roberto turned off both devices and asked, "Can you tell us Mr. Saldaña what happened that interrupted the video?"

"Yes, Pablo, whose real name was Pancho something as you just heard, was speaking when the lights went off. You have asked me not to say what he said, but I can tell you that I concluded that it was not uncommon for the lights in San Salvador to go out unexpectedly, so he had a couple of candles handy and he lit them," said Lupe, and Roberto saw that the Judge could not repress a smile at the marvelous way in which Lupe had gone around the hearsay rule.

"What happened next?" asked Roberto.

"I felt very much like going to the bathroom. I decided to go while the power came back. I asked the man where the bathroom was, he pointed to a door that cannot be seen on the screen. I went into the bathroom and closed the door behind me. I had just walked into the bathroom when I heard the front door of the small house being kicked open and a burst of machine gun fire, so I threw myself down as best as I could in the extremely small space. Then, complete silence. After a short while, I opened the door, a little at first and then fully. What I saw revolted my stomach. My man, who had been operating the video camera, was lying on the floor bleeding profusely. I walked out and found Pancho collapsed against the back of the same chair you saw him sitting on and also bleeding from several bullet wounds. I touched their neck arteries, but both were dead," finished Lupe, and his voice had an angry and somber tone.

"What happened next?" asked Roberto.

"Very carefully, I opened the door to the outside. There was nobody to be seen under the moonlight. Straining my eyes I finally was able to see the bodies of my two other men lying on the ground amidst pools of their own blood. With my gun drawn, I ran to the Jeep Cherokee in which we had arrived and called the local police requesting an ambulance. Then I returned to check my men and see if any of them was alive. Both of them were dead, they had been murdered by cutting their throats. Pancho had obviously been the target of the attack, but it shows you the savagery of this man, that to silence one man he cold-heartedly had three more killed," explained Lupe.

"You were very close to being killed yourself, right?" asked Roberto knowing full well that Lupe would take the opportunity to give testimony of the power of God.

"Yes," replied Lupe, "But praise Jesus, His angels pushed me into that bathroom."

Roberto could see the faces of those few who were in the courtroom. It seemed strange to most that such a tough man had said those words. Roberto just replied, "Yes, praise Jesus!" Then, standing up and turning to the Judge he said, "Your Honor, the defense has no more questions."

The Judge, visibly moved by the testimony, turned to Block and simply said, "Mr. Block?"

Block stood up and said, "No questions." He knew that Lupe's testimony and the presentation of the video would give the death knell to the government's case.

"Very well," said the Judge, "Bring in the jury. We are going to have to go through this once more."

After a repetition of the tape and testimony, this time before the jury, both sides closed their case and proceeded to closing arguments.

Block made a bland plea before the jury to base their verdict on the testimony of agent Carroll. Then he sat down.

Roberto stood up and said, "Just as I told you in my opening argument, the issue in this case is knowledge. Did my client know that there was cocaine in his bags?

"I submit to you that not only has the government failed to prove my client's guilt beyond a reasonable doubt, but instead, that we have proved beyond a reasonable doubt that Manolo Pardo did not know of the cocaine discovered in his bags.

"We have proved that this was a scheme devised by this mysterious man, Cesar. That in his anger and rage for what he considered to be a betrayal against his daughter, Cesar ordered his man Pancho to place cocaine in the bags that had been prepared to switch them, using the same words that Pancho used, for the real bags that my client had checked at the airport in Mexico City.

"You heard the story of Cesar in the words of Ms. Velasco. Then, the shocking testimony of Mr. Saldaña and this man called Pancho who gave you the explanation that the cocaine he put in the bags had been diluted cocaine instead of undiluted one. You remember the testimony of the Chemist. Ask yourselves, how could Pancho, hiding away in a Central American country, know of the diluted cocaine in the bags if it were not true.

"On the other hand, the prosecutor asks what would Agent

Carroll gain for lying. I will tell you what. He is convinced that my client is guilty. That is part of his personality. That is the way his personality has been shaped by the trade in which he works. By being a law enforcement officer. So he decided that, since it was possible for Mr. Pardo to get off on reasonable doubt, why not fabricate a little confession to nail him down.

"Do not be shocked. It is done, fortunately very seldom, by officers who are otherwise honest, but who are convinced that the system is tilted in favor of the guilty. So, they decide to add just a little touch to nail the coffins of the guilty defendants. The problem is that in this case Manolo Pardo is really not guilty. Thank you."

The Judge then gave his instructions to the jury. By the time he finished it was already 12:00, so he sent the jury out to lunch asking them to be back by 1:30 and begin their deliberations.

The jury began deliberating at 1:30 that afternoon. Shortly before 2:15 p.m., the jury came back with their verdict, "Not Guilty."

EPILOGUE

CORPUS CHRISTI

I t was three months after the trial of Manolo Pardo. Roberto Duran was in Corpus Christi at the Hayden W. Head Airport. He had spent the last couple of days in Corpus trying the case of an illegal reentry into the United States. It was one of the pro-bono cases that he would take from time to time if the case really merited it. This particular one was really worth it.

His client had been caught for about the seventh time trying to enter the United States illegally to work here. He was a marvelous carpenter who could make very good money in the United States but was not able to find a job in Mexico, where he had a large family to support. His real problem was that he was very honest. Instead of doing what most undocumented aliens normally do when caught, give a false name and then sign a voluntary departure form and enter again, he always gave his real identity. Immigration Officials eventually got exasperated with him and decided to prosecute his illegal reentry as a felony.

It meant that, if convicted, he would face up to three years in jail. Roberto learned about the case through one of Houston's Magistrate-Judges and offered to represent the man. It would end up costing Roberto close to five thousand dollars, because the

Criminal Justice Act (under which the court-appointed attorneys are paid) would not pay for travel or lodging because a local Corpus Christi attorney could have been appointed instead of Roberto coming all the way from Houston. That, plus the difference between his normal hourly fee of $300 as compared to the court-appointed fee of less than one hundred dollars. But it had been worth it.

The case had been fascinating. He had won the sympathy of the jury for the carpenter and got him acquitted. Now, he would turn over the case to his former fellow law student, Elizabeth Medrano, who specialized in Immigration law. Roberto had already spoken with her and there was a strong possibility that Nacho, the carpenter-client, could stay legally with a work permit in the United States and earn a very decent living for his family with his work. Roberto felt very satisfied and content. Now, he was heading home, feeling he had completed a job well done.

As he usually did, Roberto had left for the airport with more than enough time. Now, after checking his ticket, getting his boarding pass and locating the gate from where he would be leaving, he had almost one hour to kill, so he decided to get a cup of coffee.

He walked into the coffee shop and ordered a cup of coffee. While he waited, he opened his Hartmann briefcase and pulled-out his Mac Book to review the file of a lenders liability case he was working on at the time. It was the same case that had been left on the back burner while he handled the 'Pardo Case.' Now he was actively pursuing it.

While he read a memo from one of his associates with respect to the attitude of the bank president when talks of settlement were brought up, Roberto remembered the true story told to his class by Professor John Neibel during the Property course in the University of Houston, when he was lecturing them on bailment.

It seems that there was a merchant in the eighteen sixties in a small West Texas town who would send his nine-year old son to the local bank every morning with a ten dollar bill to exchange it for pennies that were needed as change in his store. One particular morning the merchant, as usual, sent his son to the bank. But, the cashier made a mistake and gave the young kid an envelope with a new series of small gold dollar coins instead of pennies, in effect giving him one thousand dollars instead of ten.

Unaware of the difference, the young boy brought it back to his father's store. The father, upon opening the envelope, discovered the bank's mistake and, as Professor Neibel put it with his marvelous sense of humor, living in an age in which people were still honest, acted with due diligence and sent back the young boy to return the money to the bank immediately.

The young boy marched back into the bank and, sensing the importance of the matter, asked to see the bank's president instead of the same cashier that had given the envelope to him. Sent into his office, the young boy, looking up at the 'rotund curve of a well-rounded belly,' as Professor Neibel put it, told the towering man who had stood up to indicate that he had no more than a few seconds to spare attending the child: "Mr. Williams, sir, I'm sorry, sir, but your bank made a mistake, sir—"

"Billy boy, my bank never, you hear it, never, makes a mistake. Run on, go back to your father." interrupted the bank's president with a thunderous voice.

The young boy looking up to the face of the tall banker, a face he could barely see because of the big belly with the double-breasted vest, just responded: "I'm sorry, sir, and thank you Mr. Williams, sir," and left the bank.

Professor Neibel had finished the story laughing and telling them that it was rumored that the father got to keep the money because he had tendered it to the bank and his tender had been refused.

"Well," said Roberto speaking to himself, "It seems that some things never change." This jerk of the president of the bank he was suing would much rather have the bank lose at trial and get to pay over a million dollars than he himself lose face and accept the very reasonable settlement that Roberto was offering.

Roberto began dictating a memo to his staff to have the material for trial ready. Just then, he heard his cell phone ringing, he pulled it out and answered: "Hello?"

Luis Gil's voice came through as crisp and clear as if he were next door, "Roberto?"

"Hi, friend, long time no see," answered Roberto jokingly. They had been together less than two weeks before in Houston, playing racket-ball and keeping alive a friendship that began with the 'Pardo Case.'

"There is something I believe you would want to know right away." Luis voice sounded solemn.

"Yes?" Said Roberto, now a little surprised that Luis had not picked up on the joke.

"The body of Manolo Pardo was discovered early this morning. He was tortured and then murdered execution style. Three shots behind the head with a high-powered gun, probably a .357 magnum," said Luis, who continued, "And guess what, the body was slumped inside his red Porsche, which was parked just outside the garage of the house of Julieta Velasco, a few feet away from the spot where young Julieta's body was discovered."

"*Pffeeww*," went Roberto letting out all the air of his lungs, "It's awful Luis, yet somehow it does not surprise me."

"Me neither, but there is more, much more. Listen, next to his body, there was a cassette tape. The officer from the Metro Police who found the body was curious about it because the Porsche has a CD player but no cassette player. By fortunate coincidence, the Metro Police officer is a good friend of mine who knows that I work for Don Jose, so he called me as soon as they discovered the body after answering a call from a passerby that thought a man had passed out inside the car. I was at the scene in a jiffy, as you can imagine, so he shows me this cassette and we listen to it together," continued Luis while Roberto's expectation grew, "I have it here with me now, if you have time I would like for you to listen to it, can you?"

"Of course," said Roberto, "Put it on, but, aren't you worried it's an open line?"

"Not really, if anybody listens to this, who cares, here it goes."

Roberto could hear noises like that of a recorder being turned on and then a hoarse voice that he did not recognize saying: "Look, Manolo, the only thing I am seeking is justice for Julieta. I am not a vengeful man, but I always do require a payback. She was my only daughter and, you understand..." there was an answer that Roberto could not make out, probably Manolo had already received a beating.

Then the same voice continued: "...Besides, I know everything. The reason I put that stuff in your bags was because I wanted you to spend some time in jail, meditating on your crime. A few of my mules have been caught and put in the slammer for thirty or forty years, so I know that there is no parole and no early release in the American federal system. I assumed that since the Americans could not be bought by your grand-daddy's money, you would spend a good deal of time in jail. Never thought grand-daddy would hire that hot shot attorney who got you off. I thought we could scare him enough, but the guy is tough, we were not able to stop him, and he got you off."

The voice then continued, "You know, that creep of Pancho was right. It was a shame to have to waste that cocaine. We are putting it to good use by poisoning these damned gringos with the help of my Arab friends. Payback, you see. People think I do it just for the money, but they are wrong. It's payback."

"Payback for all the abuses they have subjected our peoples to. They and their friends, the Jews. How do we get our payback? By poisoning their youth, destroying the minds of a generation and pushing them to welfare. They call it the war on drugs without ever realizing that it is a war all right, but they are not waging it against drugs, we are waging it against them and they are losing it, and losing badly."

"Soon, welfare will make them broke. Millions of young minds destroyed that will never recover. Their power will disappear with their money. It's already beginning to happen."

"Americans feel that they won the cold war by bankrupting the Soviets. They are right. Only that they do not seem to understand that the same thing is going to happen to them." The voice laughed, "And who's beating them? None other than those they have oppressed for years."

Roberto's skin crawled at what he was hearing. It sure seemed right on target, a gigantic conspiracy to poison America, the only way they could get even with the 'American Satan.' A really scary thought.

There was a short pause and the voice continued, "But enough of politics now. With respect to you, the only thing I want is for you to spend some time in jail, no need to kill you, what for?"

Roberto could almost imagine what was going on through Manolo's mind at that time. He must have surely thought that if he could get out of this one alive, his grandfather could again get him out of trouble, more so if it was in Mexico.

"So," the voice continued, "Why don't you tell me the whole truth. I'll tape it and then turn the tape over to the police. Once they hear the tape you'll go to jail. No way around it, not even with grand-pa's money. Go ahead, confession is good for the soul," the voice had become soft now, persuasive, almost as the voice of a priest.

Then Roberto could hear Manolo's voice, it sounded strange, as if he were munching at something, probably he had lost some teeth: "All right, but I want to ask you first, how did you find out?"

"It wasn't hard. Contrary to what you believed, my daughter and I were very close. I sought her out soon after she graduated from High School. From then on we were very close, she would tell me everything. So, when she met you and started going out with you, I knew it right away, she told me. Not only did she tell me that, she told me of her adventure with you in Acapulco, after you both came back. Then, when you failed to come through and act like a man and marry her, naturally, she turned to me again."

"I told her not to worry, I would send her over to France, or Germany, or Italy, to spend a year, supposedly studying abroad, in reality, to have her baby and then give it for adoption. She did not want to have an abortion, she was a good catholic girl. Just went and confessed with her priest. I even told her that it was her mistake. I had told her many times that, once a man gets what he wants, seldom will he care for a girl. I know. I'm not that different myself."

"So then...?" Manolo's voice was questioning.

"So then, obviously, her plans were not to commit suicide, not at all. But go ahead, you tell me what happened," said the voice.

"Well..." Manolo was still hesitant, "...What happened was that after we broke—"

"After you left her, don't try to hide it," interrupted the voice now with an angry ring to it.

"Well... yes... I was the one who did not want to see her again, so she sent me this letter threatening me. Saying that she was going to get in touch with you and ask you to kill me."

"Did she tell you who I was?" asked the voice.

"No, but I knew that you were a powerful drug baron. I figured you were posing as a highly visible politician and that Julieta was the child of one of your mistresses."

Roberto could hear the laughter of several persons and some unintelligible comment, then the voice said: "You're a smart kid Manolo. What happened after you got her letter."

Manolo's voice clearly frightened continued: "I got really scared. She did not react like all... all the girls I had laid before—" there was a loud noise in the tape followed by a groan, obviously someone had punched Manolo. Then, Roberto could hear the same voice with a tone of authority say: "Stop, don't hit him, I want him to tell me the whole story."

Manolo, now sounding even more frightened, continued: "...I was afraid, so then decided that I had to stop her. I received the letter on a Friday. I knew that the maid in her house had the Sundays off, Julieta had told me. I also knew that her mother normally went to her golf club on Sunday morning. So I figured that if I showed up at her house on Sunday morning, nobody would know it."

"And then..." urged the voice.

"Then," continued Manolo, "I went to her house that Sunday morning, around nine-thirty. Sure enough, Julieta's car was the only one in the garage, as I could see through the side window. When I rang the bell, Julieta came to open. I asked her why was it that she opened herself and she explained that the maid had the day off and she was alone in the house. Then she wanted to know if I had received the letter that she had sent. I pretended that I had not received anything. With the mail service in Mexico the way it is, I'm sure she believed it. Then I convinced her that I missed her too much, that I could not live without her. It wasn't hard, she wanted so much to believe me..." Manolo's voice now sounded almost cynical and Roberto expected to hear more noises of a beating, but there were none. It was clear the man of the voice commanded much authority.

Manolo continued: "...I told her that I wanted to marry her and could not wait even one more day. I told her I had everything prepared with a Justice of the Peace—"

"You had everything prepared, but it was not with a Justice of the Peace, right?" interrupted the voice and Roberto felt a lump in his throat listening to the pain that even through a tape recorder was reflected in the voice of Julieta's father. He himself was a father and in spite of the type of man Cesar was, Roberto shuddered at the thought of what he had gone through.

"Yes," continued Manolo's voice, "I had emptied all the bottles of sleeping capsules and tranquilizers that my mother buys. Every time she needs a pill she buys a new bottle because she always forgets where she put the others. I figured that they could come in handy sometime, so I kept them." Manolo's voice sounded again cynical, but still afraid, while he continued, "And then Julieta went upstairs to dress, because she had opened the door in her pajamas. I told her not to tell anybody, we would just announce it to the world after we were married, so she did not tell anybody."

"You're wrong," said the voice, even hoarser now, "She called me. She had the number of my private cell phone. I was in an important meeting that morning, but she left a message in my voice mail. I recorded it afterwards. Still have the tape, do you want to hear it?" It was a command, not a question, but Manolo mumbled an assent. Then Roberto heard some noises after which there was the clear voice of a young woman saying excitedly: "Daddy, daddy, I love you, I love you! I'm the happiest girl in the world! I am going to marry Manolo! Sorry I missed you, I'll tell you all later!" The lump in Roberto's throat grew larger hearing the happiness reflected in the voice of Julieta.

Manolo's voice was now sobbing. Roberto would have preferred to think that it was because of some love that he had felt for Julieta. But he suspected that it was because, by now, Manolo must have realized that Julieta's father would not let him live, "I'm sorry..." he sobbed.

"I am sorry too," said the voice that now sounded strangely calm, "But go ahead, I want to hear how you convinced her to drink that potion you had prepared."

"Well, I had already emptied a good deal of the pills in one of two bottles of Champagne that I had in a cooler in my car. While Julieta went upstairs to change I brought the bottles in. I served one tall glass for Julieta from the bottle in which I had dissolved the sleeping pills and then I opened the other bottle that had nothing in it and served myself a tall glass also. After Julieta came down fully dressed, I told her that we had to celebrate with the Champagne, which she readily agreed to do. I also told her that we had some time because the Justice of the Peace was waiting for us until 12:30."

"So...?" urged the voice.

"After we drank the first glass I asked her if she had some grapes and cheese to eat while we drank, and she left for the kitchen. I poured another glass for her from the bottle that had the sleeping pills dissolved in it. She came back with the food and started sipping at the second cup while I ate. She did not even finish her cup before she started feeling drowsy. I told her that it was because of the excitement of the upcoming wedding that alcohol was affecting her, and ask her to lie down and rest a while. In seconds, she was asleep."

"After that, I carried her to her Mustang inside the garage and sat her in the car. I turned on the engine and closed the door to the garage and left her inside. Then, I went to her bedroom and left the rest of the same pills that I had dissolved in the Champagne all over her night stand, to give the impression that she had taken them before going to the garage and turning on the engine of her car. I did not touch those pills so there were no fingerprints on them. Then, I waited for almost forty-five minutes. I knew there was a great risk of someone coming and discovering my car, but at the same time I was afraid that, if I left, Julieta might recover enough to get out of the car and get help."

"Anyway, nothing happened. Before leaving, I walked into the garage holding my breath and could see that her eyes were half open but staring into nothing, her mouth was also open and I could not see her breathe, so I figured that she was dead."

The cruelty and cold-heartedness of the words made Roberto feel almost sick.

Now, the voice of Julieta's father had a steely inflection in the middle of his irony when he asked: "For some reason, I don't believe you felt sorry, or did you?"

Manolo's voice, scared and concerned, explained: "Well sir, she had threatened me. It was self-defense really. I was certain that you would have me killed if Julieta were to ask you to do it."

"Very intelligent conclusion. I must congratulate you about your very good planning Manolo," said Julieta's father. "But as you can imagine, after the phone call I received from her, I knew perfectly well that Julieta had not committed suicide. If she did not kill herself, the logical conclusion was that you had killed her."

He obviously turned his face away from the tape recorder because it sounded muffled when he said: "So, gentlemen, what do you think? Is this enough to convict this young man of murder?" Roberto could not understand the answers, but there were several voices that could be heard. Then the hoarse voice came back with the steely tone: "Very well then, I will tell you what we will do, Manolo. Tomorrow at dawn I am going to take you to Julieta's house and there, a few feet away from where you murdered my daughter, we will park your beautiful red Porsche. Then we will carry out your punishment, death by firing squad..."

Roberto could hear Manolo's voice pleading for mercy but the voice just kept on speaking, "...I will have the same mercy on you that you had on my daughter. I will let you sweat it out one full night. Of course, if some of my men want to have some fun with you, they are free to do it. This time, neither your fancy name nor all the money and power of your grandfather are going to save you." In the background Roberto could hear what sounded like some blows and moaning. Probably the beating had started.

Then there was a click and silence. The recorder had been turned off.

Now it was the voice of Luis that said: "Roberto?"

"Yes, Luis, here I am," answered Roberto, and then added, "What about Don Jose, does he know of the tape?"

"We heard it together this morning," answered Luis, "I asked him to come over to my office, did not want to be in his house with the possibility of the mother or the grandmother walking in on us while we heard it."

"Has he given you any instructions?" Roberto was wondering what Don Jose's reaction could be.

"No," said Luis. "I asked him if he wanted me to do something about it. He just sat there for a moment and then he said, 'No Luis, let the dead bury their dead,' and that is it, he did not add a word. We were in my private office, he just got up his chair, waved to me good-bye with watery eyes, and walked out through the door. I went home to take a bath and get dressed in a suit, when I came back to the bank office I found a note of thanks from him in my fax."

Roberto felt relieved, the matter better be put to rest. He thought it ironical that the girl's name was Julieta, just as the ill-fated lovers in Shakespeare's classic. And, just as in Romeo and Juliet, revenge would only escalate into more and more violence.

He just said: "I'm glad this is not going to continue Luis. Revenge does not make any sense."

"I agree." There was a moment in which neither of the two spoke. Then Luis said:

"Anyway, I'll be in Houston next month to give you a beating at racket-ball," Luis sounded a lot less stressed now.

"Yes, friend, but we'll see who beats who and... we will talk more at length at that time."

"Sure, we will. Bye now," said Luis.

"Bye, Luis, see you soon," said Roberto.

He punched to disconnect and, as if waiting for a cue, almost immediately he could hear the call to board his flight to Houston.

It was a Continental Express jet. Roberto loved flying on the smaller planes. The sensation of flight is more acute and they have a series of single seats on one side, which makes it very comfortable.

While he went into the small jet, thinking back on what he

had just heard, he gave a deep sigh and said to himself, "How true is the old Spanish saying that, 'the faces we can see, the hearts we do not know. '"

'Only Jesus knows the hearts,' - he thought - while praising His grace. Roberto, for one, felt very happy to know that his heart belonged wholly and absolutely to the same Lord who tells us: "I will never leave you, I will never forsake you."

ABOUT THE AUTHOR

Ramón del Villar is a lawyer, a black belt in karate, a teacher, a private pilot and an author. He recently retired from his day job as Senior Interpreter in Houston for the United States District Court for the Southern District of Texas. His nonfiction text, *An Interpreters Anatomy of a Civil Lawsuit,* is available as a bilingual resource and he is working on the next adventure of Roberto Duran, intrepid attorney.

OTHER INKLINGS TITLES

Twisted Reveries: 13 Tales of the Macabre

Twisted Reveries II: Tales from Willoughby

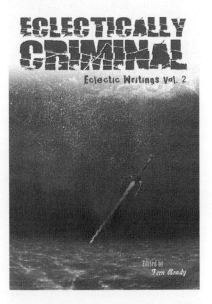

Eclectically Criminal: Eclectic Writings Vol 2

Eclectically Vegas, Baby: Eclectic Writings Vol 3

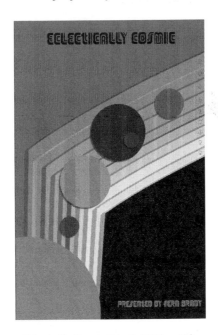

Eclectically Cosmic: Eclectic Writings Vol 4

Interpreters' Anatomy of a Civil Lawsuit

FOLLOW INKLINGS PUBLISHING BY

Signing-up for our newsletter on our website www.inklingspublishing.com

Made in the USA
Columbia, SC
26 April 2019